HAVEN'T we all read one horror story or another about someone, well, sort of like ourselves, suddenly cast into a nightmare situation that is way beyond our pampered, urban capabilities?

Every time there is a kidnapping of an innocent civilian, capture of a small boat couple by pirates, hostage situation, and on, don't we all think about how we might handle such an event for which nothing in our daily lives has prepared us?

REMAIN CALM is the ultimate extension of that "what if." This is a break neck, page-turning, belly laugh of an adventure that turns a nightmare into a Marx Brothers-level laugh fest of plot twists and the utterly un-PC and searing social satire for which Gloria Nagy has long been known.

This time, it's all set in México, combining what starts as a ten-day "soul-searching" retreat for Mimi Markow, escaping her New York City bubble and encroaching sixtieth birthday, a husband who is having a torrid affair with his iPhone and Twitter account, and kids who have drifted off into adulthood with not much time or room for mothers who do not text or tweet.

SO, against her better judgment (always a set-up for disaster), off she goes with her mysterious, glamorous, French friend Solange to open herself to the land of other options at

The Vaya Con Dios Spiritual Spa and Retreat, a la-la land filled entirely with various versions of themselves at prices fitting such desperation.

This hilarious, original, tour de force takes Nagy's scalding, clear-eyed view of life in the absolute present and pulls out all narrative stops. Fast, furious, and laugh-out-loud funny, REMAIN CALM is a look at ourselves and the astonishing way life's curve balls can turn what starts as utter terror into exactly what we need.

Nagy has been aptly compared to Tom Wolfe and Woody Allen, among others. Her ability to layer her work, combining literary illusion, keen reporting, wonderful story-telling and deep empathy, sadness, and truth under the farce on the surface, puts her own stamp on this and her other work.

Covering everything from sex, seniors, salsa, and the stress of twenty-first century reality, here she just goes for it. This is a "*poquito*" novel, without a metaphor or narrative drive to spare.

Warning, if you read it on an airplane, take some of Mimi's excess duct tape for your mouth. Laughing out loud mid-air is ill-advised.

.

REMAIN CALM

A poquito novel
by
Gloria Nagy

Sheer Bliss Communications, LLC

Remain Calm

Published by Sheer Bliss Communications, LLC.
Author services by Pedernales Publishing, LLC.

ISBN 978-0-9679436-3-3
0-9679436-3-9

For Vanessa, whose presence in the world has always been the sunshine in my heart. I.L.Y.

For Joshua, my brilliant Storm King, who inspired this and keeps my humor, pencil, and spirit sharp with his daily missives. I.L.Y.

ACKNOWLEDGEMENTS

I want to thank my husband Richard Wurman for the editing, cover creating, and anchoring only he can give; Rebecca Rex for pulling it all together; Carin Ahfeldt for making my life so lovely I can do this at all; Jim Bruno for all the sage techno, e-book and 21st-century publishing info that has been so essential (his super-charged energy was not bad, either); Barbara Ardinger for her superb copy-editing; Jose Ramirez for his passion, expertise, intelligence and care; and Life itself for providing an endless goodie box of human foibles and situations to plunder.

GLORIA NAGY

is a novelist and screenwriter. She is the author of ten novels including the best-selling *A House in the Hamptons.* Her critically acclaimed novel *Looking for Leo* was adapted as a mini-series for CBS. Her novel *The Beauty* is set in Newport and Cape Cod and has been called "a terrific fable about the futility of  escape, the inevitability of evil, and the power of redemption." She is currently working on an independent film adaptation of her novel *Virgin Kisses* and a musical review for women entitled *Where Do I Go Now?* Her latest novel is *SeaSick.*

Gloria Nagy is a member in good standing of the Authors Guild, Author League, and the Screenwriters Guild of America. She has been interviewed on social issues by Nightline. She has appeared frequently on television and has done over a hundred radio interviews on subjects relating to her work and how her themes intersect the zeitgeist. Critics have called her "the social chronicler of her time" and "the female Tom Wolfe" for her ability to "stick pins in all the hot-air balloons." Her opinions and observations have been expressed in reviews and articles for national magazines such as *Lears, Traveler, Self* and *Cosmopolitan*, as well as in speeches and writing seminars.

Her novels have been published around the world and translated into numerous languages including German, Japanese, Hebrew, Russian, and Dutch.

Titles by Author:

Virgin Kisses, Warner Books/Penguin International, 1978

Unapparent Wounds, William Morrow & Company, Inc., 1981

Natural Selections, Villard Books, 1985

Radio Blues, St. Martin's Press, 1988

A House in the Hamptons, Dell Publishing, 1990

Looking for Leo, Delacorte Press, 1992

Marriage, Little, Brown and Company, 1995

The Wizard Who Wanted To Be Santa, Sheer Bliss Communications LLC, 2000

The Beauty, Peter Mayer/Overlook Press, 2001

SeaSick, Jorge Pinto Books, June, 2009

Ms. Nagy lives in Newport, Rhode Island, with her husband Richard Saul Wurman. They have four children, six grandchildren, and three dogs, Abraham, Isaac, and Jacob.

"It looked insanely complicated and this was one of the reasons why the snug plastic cover it fitted into had the words Don't Panic printed on it in large friendly letters."

Douglas Adams, *The Hitchhiker's Guide to the Galaxy*

CHAPTER UNO

No. No. No. Shit, Shit. OH SHIT! This isn't happening! I'm dreaming it. No. NO, I'm not, because if I was dreaming it, this is the place where I always, always wake up, always, like clockwork and have to pee and take a pill because I'd never go back to sleep, which is hard enough to do in the first place. Oh my God. Oh, MY GOD.

Breathe. Breathe, Mimi. Remember, you must remember. Focus.

So where was I? I was walking down the hill from the yoga center to the midnight meditation seminar. Yes. It was chilly.

Not supposed to be chilly in México in the summer. I was not happy. So what else is new. I was really not happy and feeling like a victim and forgetting all my mantras, schmantras, and not acting like a victim script and not blaming other people like my so-called soul-sister Solange (what happened to you, Mimi? Who would head off to eco-schmecko woo-woo retreat-land with someone named Solange. I mean. SOLANGE?) You knew better. You knew she doesn't look at life from your POV. She thinks I'm cynical. I'm not cynical; I'm just realistic and hopefully wary.

Yes, so, where was I. Fucking Solange! I hate meditation. I hate organized woo-woo. I hate yoga. I really hate being in México without margaritas and guacamole. And, besides, avocados and agave are supposed to be very good for you.

You're wandering. Do not wander off. You've been kidnapped!

You are locked in a closet. You are blindfolded, and your mouth, wrists, and ankles are taped. You have no idea how you got here or who did it. I was walking, and then there was a rustle and then I felt a pricking pain, more like stabbing, really, and now I'm awake and I'm—why aren't I terrified?

Must be shock. I'm in shock. I must be in shock! Good, I think shock is good. Because otherwise, knowing me, I'd be hysterical, and if you get hysterical with tape over your mouth, you could choke to death or strangle on your tears or phlegm. Shock is good. Numb, good. Better stay this way. I'm agoraphobic. I'm claustrophobic. I have a professionally-documented, generalized anxiety disorder, clinically documented, and I'm not hysterical? Shock, for sure.

So, what else do I remember? SHIT. Where's my purse? I can handle anything if I have my purse. My meds, my moisturizer, my estrogen, my inhaler, my gummies, my breath mints, my hair ties, my phone. My phone! They have probably stolen my entire identity (such as it is). My lip gloss. This is not good, really not good.

Cannot blame Solange. Well, I can, but it's self-defeating. All that therapy, and I'm blaming her like crazy. How did I let *her talk me into this? What was the matter with me? Well, that's a ticket to the Closed Lane. Did they take her, too? Did she plan this? I mean, she is French and her ex-husband is Mexican. Maybe she has a secret life outside of Palm Beach and New York. Maybe her former husband, who she's so vague about, is a drug lord or a professional kidnapper. I'm a hostage! I'm a kidnap victim in México, where they disembowel women, cut their bras off, and hang them from bridges! Ears and thumbs. They cut off ears and thumbs of innocent children and hold them for $50 ransoms!*

No, no, no. Mimi, don't go there. Think about John McCain. Think about Lawrence and the kids. (Isn't that what everyone who's been kidnapped and lives to tell says they did?) Well, that's what they say, but I have a feeling that comes later, like after they've been in captivity for awhile and have gotten over the shock and maybe been moved to a small, dark room and are chained to a bed and their mouth is un-taped and they have had access to a shower and their Xanax. HOLY SHIT! I'm in a closet, locked in a closet by unknown assailants, and all because I let fucking Solange talk me into this "journey into your deeper being."

Vaya con Dios Holistic Eco-Healing Spa and Retreat! Everything I hate. This is Talmudic justice for not trusting my gut. I could have taken a cruise with Lawrence. Well, maybe not, maybe (do try and be honest, here, Mimi, since you may have only a short time left to be anything). The idea of this was to take a time-out from Lawrence and marriage and everything that was driving you crazy and seek peace. Not that I know much about peace, seek though I have; it was my statement about putting my needs first (that last session with Chloe Schlongstein). Sad enough to entrust my decision-making process to someone named Chloe Schlongstein, no matter how many degrees she has on her wall.

Focus, I have to focus. My mouth itches like crazy. Maybe this is good for wrinkles when they rip it off, like waxing? I have to pee, now I really have to pee. And I'm starving. Can that be normal? I don't think I'm supposed to be hungry and thinking about carnitas with melted cheese and onions when I'm a kidnap victim. Doesn't sound very noble. Maybe a side of frijoles negros and pico de gallo.

Maybe I'm not in a closet. I don't smell clothes, but maybe Mexican closets smell different. I wonder if John McCain was blindfolded. What is it with you and John McCain? He's your kidnap role model? He was a POW! And all you know is what he said happened. You don't really KNOW what kept him "sane" (and sane? Where did you get the idea he was sane?) For all you know, when he wasn't being tortured, he might have kept going by playing tic-tac-toe with dead flies and masturbating. Whew. That would be a lot of dead flies and a lot of…. I think this is what Dr. Schlongstein would call an "unproductive line of thought."

Why would anyone kidnap me? I'm nobody. Well, I mean, I'm somebody to my family and a few friends and people I pay for grooming and donate money to and Abel (dogs count). Abel thinks I'm somebody. But then, he loves anyone who feeds him and scratches his butt. No, Abel cares about me. Why did I name him Abel of all things? Biblical is fine, but a victim name like Abel? Should have named him David or Solomon or George Clooney. I know he isn't in the Old Testament, but he's most certainly not a potential victim type.

So think of a reason. Lawrence is tired of me and wants out and doesn't want to pay for thirty-five years' worth of togetherness. Hmmm. Our kids don't want to wait for us to go naturally and have concocted a scheme beginning with my disappearance in México and ending with their father's faked suicide. Abel wants a bigger bed and…. This is not helping, but, then again, why ME? Mimi, you funny little good for nothing, Mimi…. Can't be the right lyrics. Maurice Chevalier would not sing to those lyrics. You are being so mean to yourself. This is not going to help you figure this out.

What's right in front of you? Deep Throat it! Follow the money. You have money. Well, you have Mr. and Mrs. Money. Maybe not a lot of money by the new money standards or by Mexican billionaire standards, but compared to the "Give me fifty dollars and I'll not cut off your toddler's other ear" standards, you're rolling in it.

But how would they know? It had to be someone who works at the Retreat! An inside job! But still. Every woman there fits that bill. So what am I missing here? Oh, God, I really have to pee. And it's so hot in here. This is not good, I need to re-focus and not think about my bladder or a great big quesadilla with lots of melted cheese and fresh salsa with cilantro and a Corona with a big hunk of lime. On a huge plate. None of that small plate trendy bullshit. Another tragedy of techno-mania. No one has enough attention span to concentrate on one plate of food…. Lots of little saucers coming fast.

Wait. Wait. I moved my lips. Salivating, maybe? The duct tape is moving. My sweat is loosening it. Probably not high-quality duct tape, probably not high-quality kidnappers. Probably bought it at some border city Costco place on sale. Probably use A LOT of it. Aha! I can push my tongue out. If I can really push, I think I can pull my lips out. Push, push, Mimi, remember childbirth. Push the fucker. Yes. It's working. It's not a movie. I'm really doing this. Thank you, God, for poor quality duct tape!

I'm free! What a relief. So now what do I do? If I call out, is that in my best survival interests? Oh, boy, how great this feels, to move my mouth. To breathe through my mouth! I will never take such small blessings for granted again. Oh, sure, I've heard that one before.

Now what? Think, Mimi! My hands must have the same tape. I can use my teeth now and my tongue. Yick. The kidnappers have touched the tape and God only knows where else it's been.... Just do it! Okay. Okay. Movement. Unbelievable. I am freeing myself! Yes! Hands! Hello, my little Russian Jewish hands. I love you!! I will never take you.... Never mind. Now the blindfold. Shit! It is a closet. No clothes. Some dirty...what are those things? Better not look too closely. Now what?

Take it slow. Don't think about your bladder. Don't think about soft corn tortillas with melted butter. Go back to "follow the money." Hmm, not a clue. I wonder if they've called Lawrence? Oh, boy. Now I'm scared. Now the shock is wearing off. What will he do?

Half the time, I don't even think he knows I'm there, anyway. "She's gone? Naw. She's somewhere in the house." I think I've lost Lawrence. He's in love with his iPhone. Cheating with the phone.

Obsessed with it. I see him smiling at it when he's looking at his mail. A very unnerving, kind of lecherous smile, like THEY both share a secret. I just so don't get it.

It's like those pod people movies, when suddenly the people you knew best show up and they are not the same. They look the same, but they ARE NOT the same. Social Networking, Oy. (I still think there are three networks and they all have initials and programming.) Twitter, schmitter. Once you've Twittered, are you a twat? Facebook. LinkedIn? Is that one? Lawrence is on everything. EVERYTHING. And when he's not "networking," it's video games. Zombies and sharks attacking, like Jacob plays. But he's four! I think "Grandpa" learns them from him. And all that reverent dependence on the computer geniuses; who have rendered us helpless and Paleolithic when, really now, who are these kids but the TV repairmen of the twenty-first century?

And all that phone Solitaire? I don't get solitaire. So depressing. Just the name. Sort of like admitting you can't find anyone to play cards with. Isn't playing cards supposed to be about schmoozing? Not being solitare-y? What stops you from cheating? I don't know. I wish I could understand it all. So boring! Who cares!!!! He has 2,000 Facebook "Friends". Puh-leeze. He only actually knows about 70 of them and that's a "pushing it" list. He probably, actually likes maybe ten of them. Maybe one of them planned this? Some Facebook/Twitter kidnap cartel. Knows us, knows I was going on this trip, he blabs all kinds of things on his Twitter.

Not that I really know what they do, but anything that eliminates all punctuation and makes everyone sound like a semi- literate preschooler can't be good. "how r u? i am going to bake a potato now."

Lawrence. Makes me so sad. Retirement is a joke. Yak. Yak. Yak. All day on the phone. On this committee and that committee and this "board" and that one. He even has a book club! A book club for men! I don't know. I must be small-minded. Hair Club for Men I can understand. Book clubs seem more like a girl thing. Drink a little wine, gossip, maybe read a few pages. Reading is too important for book clubs.

Yak. Yak. Yak. Besides, 80 percent of everything anyone talks about now is bullshit 90 percent of the time…or 90 percent is, 80 percent of the time or…Lawrence can shovel it, good for him. He's home and I never see him. Maybe it is him? Maybe he does want me to go, but…no way. He's too scared of me. But if they called him and said—maybe I could ask them to do this, make them a better offer? "If you call my husband and tell him you don't want any money, you'll release me and all you want is one thing. He surrenders his phone. Your wife for your phone," and see what he says? I could up the ante and test him.

What if he chooses the phone? Oh, God, I'm crying. There it is, scratch a kidnap victim, and out comes all the fear. I've seen all those 48 Hours *and* Dateline *shows. The wives and children of kidnap victims mortgage their houses and quit their jobs and deplete their savings to search for their beloved moms and pops and hubs and wives and everything.*

What is the truth here? Why aren't I calling out to someone, really? Maybe because I don't truly believe any of them love me enough to do that. Maybe a little, but they'd put a limit on it, like a sub-prime house bid. "We'll go up to a 150 thou, but after that, I don't know, we're very busy and we don't really need her that much anymore, anyway...."

Oh, boy, Mimi, you had better search around and see if your purse is in here. You are definitely on a bad path. This is not why you've spent a small fortune enabling Dr. Schlongstein to look far more glamorous than you, yourself, to veer off into the Badlands. This is not a "productive line of thought."

Okay. Take a couple of deep breaths. In and out. I can see a little bit of light under the door. There's a knob. What if it's not locked? Would they be that lame? Well, they think I'm taped up and probably still out cold, so if I get on my knees and very quietly try the—uh oh. What was that sound? Breathing? Scratching? There is something in here with me and it's alive!!!

Oh, shit! A rat. I bet it's a huge Mexican rat with rabies or bubonic plague. Oh, God, anything but a rat! I'm going for the door, I'll take my chances with the human rats, ohhhhh, it's moving! Turn the knob, Mimi, turn it now!

It's open! It's not locked. I'm up. I'm out. No one's here? Shut the closet door! Did they leave? Uh oh, a man is running at me! Is that a knife in his belt?

"Help! I need help!"

"Please. Please! No! No look at me. Momento. Un momento!!!

He's running the other way? What is he doing? He's getting something out of his pocket. Oh, uh oh. A ski mask? He is putting on a ski mask! He's the kidnapper!!!

"You frighten me! You must no see me. Is bad. Very bad. I no expecting you to come out!"

"I frightened YOU? You have the knife, the ski mask. I'm the kidnap VICTIM! I've been locked in a closet with a big rat, held hostage, bound with duct tape, and I frightened YOU?"

"Closet no is locked."

"Oh, perdóneme! Let's not quibble. "

"You all taped. So, I no think I need to lock the closet."

"Well, about that. I know this is not advice you will most likely take, just like my kids never do, but what the hell. Lousy tape. Since in your line of work, tape is, like, a very big deal, this is not where you should cut costs. Comprende? Go for the good stuff. Bet you got it at Costco in bulk."

"Walamart."

"Even better. How about this. Why don't we take a little trip back to Walamart together. You can blindfold me, whatever works, and I can be your witness. Demand a refund. Tell them, their cheap tape cost you a good ransom deal. I mean, after all, they have some responsibility. But in the future, I'd spring for the good stuff."

"You are making a joke on me."

"I'm being sarcastic. I am sarcastic. Maybe that's why

someone wanted to kidnap me and stuff me in a closet with a big, disease-carrying RAT!"

"No rat. I am clean hombre. No rat en mi casa. It's Taco."

"Taco? Well, unless there are some new culinary traditions down here, I have never seen a taco that breathes!!!"

"No, not a taco. Taco. A little perro. His name is Taco. I put him with you for the comfort."

"Very simpático. I'm now supposed to thank you, because when I'm taped up and blindfolded and locked in a closet...."

"No locked."

"Okay. Sorry. Makes it more dramatic, don't you think? Okay, shoved in a closet, drugged, and kidnapped. Boy, having something breathing and scratching really was comforting. Muchas gracias."

"I get him out now. He is muy nervioso, because of his kidnapping."

"You kidnapped a dog named Taco, también! Are you a madman?"

"No, no. I no kidnap him! The bad kidnappers do it with the little girl."

"Ah ha, well, I think the shock is now wearing off. I, donde esta mi purse? Uh, mi bolsa? I think my blood sugar just dropped down to my pies and I may be having a panic attack. Medicina en mi bolsa."

"Sí. Sí. In the closet. I get your bolsa and Taco."

"Good. Very bueno. I'm going to sit on this chair. Okay?"

"Sí. Sí. But put it by the closet, so I can see you. I no want you behind me."

"No problema. That's nice. I finally got to say that to

someone where it actually applies."

"Okay, I get Taco and the bolsa. You sit aquí. I need to find the tape, también. I appreciate what you say. Estúpido, to buy cheap tape. But I have no money, and my familia use all the good tape."

"Oh, that's too bad. So many victims, so little quality tape left. What is that!!! Oh my God! What happened to him?"

"No, no. Don't be scared. Is Taco, is okay. He very nervioso."

"His ear is missing!!! Oh, God! You cut his ear off!!! Is it a Chihuahua?"

"Sí. Chihuahua, but, no I no do it. It was, I say to you, but I should not say it, the bad kidnappers, when the parents of the girl no pay fast, they send it."

"Hello! Hola! How would they think some random puppy ear had anything to do with their little girl?"

"Because it is her perro and they send her ear, too."

"Oh, God, please, my bolsa. I think I'm going to faint, have an asthma attack, a massive anxiety attack and hypoglycemia and die right here."

"No. No. Señora. No die. I sorry, I speak too much. I don't do this thing. I save the dog, I name him. I keep him for my niños. No be scared. I never hurt nobody. Here. Here is your purse? English word, no? Perdóneme, I have to check, make sure you have no weapon. I looking, okay. I must take your phone. Here, is bolsa."

"Thank you. I'm going to have a piece of dulce now and take a puff on my inhaler. See? And this is a tranquilizer? Comprende? Want one?"

"No, gracias. I must be alert."

"Hmm. Good point. Me, too. Just the inhaler and the candy and a little face cream. Okay?

"Soooo, now, one more thing. I am about to pee pee in my pantalones. Is there a baño. May I por favor use the baño?"

"Yes. Yes, I take you. You go before me, down this hall. I forget about ladies and pee pee. Since my wife die, I no think of it so much."

"I'm very sorry for your loss. Can you close the door? Por favor?

"Sí. I give you privacy. It is clean. I am clean man."

No rats, just a one-eared Chihuahua and, yes, I see Ajax and Windex and Lysol. Name brands, no generics except for the, not to beat a dead…well, the tape. *It is clean. No window. Only a little high up air vent, can't get out from there. Mimi put some paper down and just pee. I could take the Lysol and spray him in the eyes. He's wearing a ski mask! You can't even see his eyes. He's so sweet….* **Shit!** *I've got Stockholm Syndrome! That's how suggestible I am. I've only been talking to him for, like, fifteen minutes and I'm already on his side. Dead wife. He saved the* *little dog! Oy. Time to start saying a lot of long forgotten Yiddish expressions left over from somewhere. What to do?*

"Señora. Is time now. If you are finish?"

"Sí. But if I could just, maybe brush my teeth and freshen up a little? Maybe a shower? I'm much, much less sarcastic when I'm clean. Uh, limpia."

"Sí. I will do it, but it take some time. I must wait for hot agua. Only in afternoon. Dos horas. Okay?"

"Okay, like what if it wasn't?"

"That's funny. You are funny lady."

"Under normal circumstances, I'm hilarious."

"Sí. This not normal circumstances. I like this word. We go back to kitchen, now. Back to the chair. I must put more tape upon you."

"Sure. Just not my face, I need air to stay calm. Okay? And food. Is there any food? My blood sugar, I get very mean when yo tengo mucho hambre."

"You speak good Spanish."

"No, only la escuela. Muchas años pasado y muchas vacaciones en México, though this is the last one, I can promise you, even if I keep my ears."

"Do not say. México is beautiful country. Do not let one bad experience…."

"Like being kidnapped? Nah. What a thought."

"You are being sarcastic now?"

"Absolutamente."

"Is very sad. You think I am bad man. I do very bad thing. But I am not a real kidnapper. This my first time. But my wife, she die, because the drugs for her cancer, too much dinero and

I have cuatro niños and my little boy, he have problem with his heart and he need operación. I no know what to do. I am poor."

"Listen, Señor, whoever you are, I'm sure ski masks go with no names, but do you think it's fair to lay the mutilated puppy—"

"No puppy. He is old. Diez años. Lo mismo as the little girl."

"All Chihuahuas are puppies to me, but *WHATEVER*. The point here, a really major point for me, is *YOU* are the bad man. *I* am the terrified victim of a plot. I am also the kind of person, and you may not understand most of this, but, then again... I am what is known as a 'co-dependent personality'. Comprendre?"

"No comprendro."

"Tough toastados. I am a person who tends to put the lives of other people in front of my own, which in this extremely and rapidly accelerating century of self-centered, narcissistic Twitter Twits, makes life hard enough, just trying to remember I count, too and not act like a, well, *victim*. *So* this whole thing (kidnap VICTIM. Why me?) is muy mal por mi recovery. Comprende?"

"No comprendo anything but, recovery from qué?"

"Birth. Comprende?"

"A little."

"Anyway, I'm basically talking to myself to calm down, so it's okay. I do it with my shrink, too."

"Shrink? Like to be made smaller?"

"Hmm. I think you've hit on something very importante. I like your question. Where was I?"

"You were talking about thinking too much about other personas, not being nice to yourself first."

"I said that?"

"No, I just think it is what you are meaning."

"Not bad. How would you like to move to New York, change your name to Schlongstein, and be my therapist."

"This is sarcastic, verdad?"

"Only partly. Anyway, the point of this is, how can I say this nicely, YOU CAN'T LAY YOUR DEAD WIFE, FOUR STARVING CHILDREN, ONE WITH A BAD HEART, MUTILATED OLD CHIHUAHUA, AND WHAT A GOOD GUY YOU ARE ON ME!!! Now I'm feeling sorry for you and worrying about what will happen to your family if you get caught and go to jail and how much dinero you need to pay for your kid's operación and, I really need to concentrate on how I GET THE FUCK OUT OF HERE and what you want and who hired you and if you're going to hurt me. Just a few little things like that. So it is really a whole lot easier for me to only see your knife and terrifying ski mask and not think about your life outside of this SITUATION. Comprende?"

"Sí. Sí. I understand this. I make so many mistakes. I should not talk with you at all. They say no talk with her. And I tell you so many things. You, I no know why, but you are a kind woman, you have very kind eyes and make me feel like I can hablar con usted and I make big mistakes, it is not your fault. Not your concern."

"Oh, that's better. Now I feel like a horrible person!"

"No. You not. You good lady. I no hurt you. It's only my family. They are very mean men. I afraid they will find out I talk with you and you get out of closet and they will come."

"The bad kidnappers are your *family* members?"

"Sí. For many years. My uncle and my brother and my two cousins. Many kidnappings. They make a lot of money. They work for the cartels, también."

"Oy vey. That isn't Spanish."

Breathe, Mimi. If you're not going to take a Xanax, you must keep breathing and remain calm and keep him talking.

"So, uh, let me try to understand this. Your family members, the men, anyway, are professional kidnappers and drug dealers. But you are a good guy, just burdened with a lot of big problemas and muchos niños and no dinero and so they let you have a little pesca, me, to try you out?"

"Sí. But I say only this one time. Just to get the money for my son. And no to hurt you."

"I am SO relieved. I'm also kind of curious, since this may not go so well. I mean, don't you have sort of an income tax thing and an unemployment insurance thing in México? What happens between kidnappings? Do your relatives go down to collect unemployment benefits and write "professional kidnappers" where it says occupation? What would the person who decides on the payments ask them? 'How many kidnap attempts have you made since your last claim?'

"And they might say perhaps, 'We are trying our best, but things are tough. Every rich person has security systems and bodyguards and bulletproof cars and huge walls around their houses, and the poor people, the quick little jobs, don't pay enough. It's a jungle out there and more and more competition all the time.'

'Well, I sympathize señors, but I'm afraid you're going to have to try harder. Think about widening your victim base. I need to see some serious attempt for the record or no more benefits.'"

"You are being sar—"

"Fucking-A. Excuse my language. I don't want you to stop thinking I'm a nice lady, but this is ridiculous! Where are your parents? Are they drug dealers and kidnappers, too?"

"No, no, they were simpatico. Hard workers. Life too difícil, too much burdens. They die young. We have to make our way."

"Oh, no, sorry I asked. Here we go again. Now I feel responsible for your entire family!"

"No, no. Do not think that. They are bad men. You are lucky I am your kidnapper."

"Now, *that's* funny. Okay then, here goes. I have to ask about the little girl, Taco's owner. What, um, exactly did they do with her? Is she here somewhere?"

"No, no. That was a big, muy importante ransom. Very much money. She was from very rich familia in Cuernavaca. It was in the U.S. periodicós, también. They ask for many millions of dollars, and the authorities, they think they can find her, but my uncle get mad and he send Taco's ear and then, because, like you say, they don't know for sure it's her perro, they send her ear, very bad thing and then they get the money very quick and she go home."

"Without her dog?"

"She no want him, no more. She say he 'give her the creeps,' bad memories. So I ask my uncle if I can keep him."

"You're kidding? Now I'm on their side. Wonder how she'd have felt if Mom and Dad decided she gave *them* the creeps, no longer perfect, can't wear those little pearl earrings they must have given her for Christmas. No more ponytails. Unbelievable!

"Maybe there should be a list of people who deserve to be kidnapped. You could probably jump start the entire economy and lower the need for cutting all the waste and corruption out of Pemex and your government and stop all those poor illegals from risking their lives to go to America and do everything no one else wants to do and.... Sorry. I got carried away."

"You know so much about my country. I am impressed."

"I don't know very much about anything. I just read a lot and remember poco about many things that drive me loco. Comprende?"

"Sí. Injustices make you loco."

"Right on. I really do think you could be my Médico Scholongstein, if we could only do something about the, uh, ski mask."

"Is very hot and make a rash on my face, but is necesario, you could recognize me. I sorry, but if I remove it, I must blindfold you again and also I forget to tape your hands."

"No, no. Then I can't eat and I really am getting light headed. I have no idea how long I've been here."

"Not so long."

"And not so long in Spanish, means?"

"Only dos días."

"Two days!!! I was out for two days! What did you stick in me, the Michael Jackson drug?"

"No, not so bad. My sister is a nursing estudiante. We so proud of her. She give me the medicina and show me how. Not to hurt you, only to make you sleep."

"Well, give the señorita an A for the semester. I never knew they taught nursing students how to render kidnap victims unconscious as one of their courses. Muy impressive."

"You are being…."

"You can now safely assume, I am being the S word pretty much of the time. So, please, please, since both you and I are making this up as we go along, now, you understand?"

"Sí. Sí, I do. Nothing is going how I think. How they tell me."

"Well then, since we both, in a way have the same goal. Neither of us wants your Bad Kidnapper relatives to kill us, I think we have to be amigos, sort of?"

"I think you are correct."

"So that means trusting one another un poco. So, por favor. If you open mi bolsa, you will see some eyeglasses and if you look through them you will see that I am very, muy, muy short-sighted. Blind as an Acapulco cave bat without them. Did I not have glasses on when you stuck a needle into my neck so expertly?"

"Sí. I have them in my pocket."

"Well, take them out and see for yourself. The point is, if you don't get too close to me, I would never be able to describe you as anything more than, and I'm profiling here, very un-PC, but screw that, a medium tall young man with black hair, dark eyes and light brown skin, which we can safely say also fits about 25 million or so of your fellow countrymen."

"Sí. I am looking. You have very bad eyesight. Like mi niña, she only siete años, but she wear very big glasses, other kids make jokes about it, call her names…"

"Oh, no, no. Remember? Do not lay any more of this on

me and I promise, I won't tell you about my childhood? Deal?"

"Sí. Deal."

"So I'll stay way over here on my chair, and you can take off that really disturbing, serial killer mask."

"Okay. But I no killer. I not a…."

"Bad man. I agree."

"Gracias. Is so much more comfortable without this thing."

"And, just a thought. If you got it at Walamart with the tape? You might think of upgrading to something less rough and heavy, maybe a nice cotton, since, again, it's a business expense."

"You are, okay being that S word, is funny, and verdad. It was on sale."

"So now then, maybe you will tell me your llamo? You know mine. I will swear on the lives of my dog, grandchild, and children that I will not ever tell anyone your name or that I saw you or anything. I do believe you are a nice guy who is desperate, and we need to help one another. I want you to get the money you need and not make your relatives mad at you, and I want to get out of here and be taken back to where you found me as soon as possible."

"Sí. Sí. I only have to wait until my uncle, he say he has the money and then I take you and he never know nothing."

"Okay, Señor. Now, about something to eat?"

"Oh, perdóneme. I have something very nice. Special burritos, very fresh, pollo y queso fresco y salsa verde. My tía, she have a stand. She make the best ones in Vera Cruz."

"Vera Cruz??? Where they recently found thirty-five mutilated bodies of drug dealers and murderers dumped by the side of the highway? That's where we are!!!"

"No. No. We not so close to that road. That was next to the big mall in Boca del Río. Much trouble, but it is bad men killing other bad men. Not to worry about. And that was the first time, very bad, but it is a muy hermoso place, many good people."

"Next to the mall! I think I need to put my head between my legs for a minute. If you would make the burritos, I'll just take a little time out to have a panic attack. Gracias."

"I cook. It will make you feel better. And my relatives, they did not do this one."

"Very reassuring. Oh, boy. Do you have a paper bag? If I'm not taking a pill, maybe I should breathe into a…."

"No papel. Only plastico."

"Not a good alternative. Never mind. I no talk now, okay?"

"I cook. You will like this and it will make you happy."

"Well, since ten years of Dr. Schlongstein, and life itself have failed to achieve that, bring on the burritos."

CHAPTER
DOS

I am not going to faint. I am not going to. Think, Mimi. Press your thumb into the back of your neck. Yes! Where did I hear that? It brings blood pressure up. Wow. It's working. I'll sit up and keep my eyes closed and breathe. This is a lot of incoming. He's humming. He's actually humming while he's cooking me lunch? This is very confusing.

What is the good news here? (Always a pony in the shit pit. Good old woo-woo touch might work here.)

Good news, he really does seem to be harmless and not evil, almost too innocent about what is really happening, but then again, maybe that's part of his schtick. To throw me off. Like Ted Bundy and the fake cast and the puppy dog eyes... Gotta get some Neosporin out of my purse, that dog's ear looks infected.

So, Mimi, I am very impressed with you. Some balls, big cojones you're showing. Not all quivery (well, quivery but not passive/victim quivery, not at all) good job! Almost cunning, never knew I had cunning in me, but he's opening up more and more, so that's good. Now, what's not good?

EVERYTHING ELSE! Clearly it's his very scary relatives who are behind this...ah, behind what? Have they called Lawrence and demanded ransom? He said he was waiting for a call from his uncle. Uncle sounds really evil. I'm beginning to see not having any living extended family members as a good thing. No one's called. No one's demanded to hear my voice before they pay the money?

Two days I've been here? Ay, chihuahua (what movie was that from?) This just doesn't make sense. Thirty-five bodies dumped next to the MALL. What about any of this makes sense?

My phone hasn't rung, either! Not like Lawrence is burning up the wires, though. It's probably totally discharged, no battery power left, so....

    He's got to put me back in the closet at some point, or they'll know, so I have to make a move before then, when his guard is down and he's really trusting me. I've never in my entire life betrayed a trust (not that I can remember, anyway). If they blame him, he won't be able to raise his kids and his son will die and... SHIT! I knew this was going to happen. He has to come with me. Oh, good, Mimi, I'm sure the police will pat him on the back and give him a nice big reward. This is not a Jennifer Aniston movie! The police are either on his uncle's team or they will arrest him for kidnapping or he'll escape and go home and his family will murder him and toss him out of a moving truck next to Burger King or Taco Bell or The Gap or some place.

    So if Lawrence pays and the relatives come to set me free and I'm back in the closet when they show up, then they won't know and I'll go home like the little spoiled brat, but then again, these are very bad guys, and what if Lawrence can't raise enough money or doesn't try hard enough…not back to that, are we. I'm doing so well here. Two days? In the movies, they always call and make the demand right away or pretty soon. Anxious family members hovering around the phone. FBI agents looking grim and steely in the background. Something doesn't make sense here.

Hello Earth to Mimi. How about NONE of it makes sense! There were celebrities there! People who flew in on their private jets to worship at the feet of Mr. Vaya con Dios himself. What's his name? Jesus, Of course it is! What? Something not very Mexican sounding. Seriously rich women and men. Paying $10,000 a week to drink cucumber juice and sleep in cement bunkers. What a crock of…. Quite a profit margin. Everyone's crazy! I could have stayed home to drink cucumber juice in the privacy of my own kitchen. You're wandering again, Mimi. Focus and focus fast. Umm, those burritos smell fantastic….

"I am going to come close to you now, so por favor, no look at me. Is important to eat it very hot and I make some arroz and frijoles and there is special salsa. You will feel more relaxed after this."

"My eyes are closed. Tell me when I can look."

"Ahora. I will eat by the sink."

"Oh my God! This is amazing. Fántastico! There's something more in this. The seasoning is incredible."

"You know good food! Yes. It is my tía's secret ingredients, she no tell nobody. She say it will be buried with her. When mi madre was dying, she…"

"Remember our deal? First, I at least eat this wonderful comida before we go back to, you know, the subjects that make me feel sorry for usted?"

"Sí. Sí. I am regretful for saying it. I feel like you are my friend. And I have no one to talk to for so long, and…."

"I do understand. Really. But it only makes everything much more complicado for both of us."

"Sí."

"And I know this won't make sense to you, Señor, but for me to not listen to your problems, is MEGA. Screw Dr. Schlongstein. All I really needed was a positive hostage situation."

"I no think you are hostage. That is different."

"Hmm. You're right. You know, your tía, I could bring her to New York and introduce her to some muy importante restaurant people and she could market these and bring money for your family. I own a little boutique cooking ware store, so I know many people in the food industry and…. Forget I just said that. Shit! I was doing so well."

"Sí. I forget. I no think she go, anyway. She very, how you say, not good with strangers."

"Shy."

"Sí. Shy, like mi niña with the bad eyes."

"They used to call me names, too. 'Four eyes.' But she can

get contact lenses when she's older. I happen to hate them, but most people prefer them and, okay, we are not talking about this anymore because I was just about to recommend an eye clinic for her."

"Is not your problema. I just making the conversation. When we eat, is good to talk."

"I LOVE this food! I don't suppose, I know I shouldn't, but by any chance do you have a cold cervesa? That would be perfectamente."

"I no have. Is too much dinero. But, I have a good bottle of tequila. Very good quality.

"Beer is too expensive, but tequila isn't?"

"Oh, sí. Coca-Cola and cervesa, mucho dinero. Tequila like water here, very cheap."

"No shit."

"Is verdad. I no lie. Never. Mi padre he teach me to always say what is true and that is why the patrón he is working for at the place where they kill the pigs, there is an accident and the amigo of mi padre, he lose his arm and is not mi padre's fault, but the person who make the mistake with the machine that cut up the pig, he blame mi padre and no one believe him and he lose his job and it too much, what you say before, "injustice," and he have a bursting in his brain and—"

"Señor, you're doing it again."

"I sorry. I bring tequila. To make more happy occasion. Mi tía will be so proud that a rich American lady who is in the food business like her burritos. You should try her tamales and her chicken mole."

"Maybe she could advertise locally. 'The favorite chef of gringo kidnap victims.'"

"Now, you are being...."

"Sorry. It just slipped out. I think a poco tequila would be great."

"Here I come. Close the ojos for uno momento. I am pouring it."

"Now?"

"Sí. I have some, too. We will toast to our safe returning to your family and the healing of my son."

"Sí. Salute!"

"Salud, Señora."

"Wow! That is good! I haven't had real food, let alone booze, since I came to that damn Retreat. All they give us is vegetable juices and some kind of vitamins. So I was already very hungry, even before you, uh, took me away."

"Is not even real vegetable juices or vitamins. Jesus is not a good person."

"I knew it! I just felt it. He's a phony."

"Sí. That is the word. Rich people do not have much sense. He buy the juice and the pills at…"

"Do not say Wal-a-mart."

"No. The Costco in México City. Very cheap there."

"Oh, boy, is this going to blow my friend's mind. What's his last name?"

"Well he say his name is Jesus Pilgrim, no even Mexican name. But he no real Mexican. He is born in San Diego, California. He know my—no, no. Is tequila speaking now, I say no more."

Be cool, Mimi. Tequila is good for finding out 'why you.' Don't have anymore, keep him talking. Well, maybe just a little, man, this is great stuff, and these burritos are life-changing….

"May I have some more tequila, Señor? Just a poco. It's

making me so much more relaxed. No more panic attack."

"Sí. Sí. Is very good for the health. Just close the eyes and I pour."

"You know, I do think now that we are amigos and we have the same goal and we have shared many things, and since you know my name and I think you trust me, can you please tell me your name? Just your first name, it feels so silly to call you Señor".

"Okay. I agree. Buenos Días."

"Why would you say that? Good morning? You are making fun of me, now."

"No. Is my name. My, how you say, 'little name.'"

"Nick name?"

"Sí. Nick name. Because I was a very…."

"Good boy."

"Sí. Mi madre say I such a good boy, I should be called Buenos, and our second name is Díaz, so that is what she call me and everyone call me."

"Well, Buenos is a very nice nick name. My real name is Miriam, but my mother called me Mimi or Mim, and that's all anyone has ever called me. Miriam sounds like the name of a very boring person, don't you think? But then, you know my name."

"No. That is not your name. Is not what you say."

"No more tequila for usted. Of course it's my name. Mimi. Miriam Markow. Hello? Don't they write down the kidnap victim's name and give you a picture and description? Otherwise you'd be grabbing all the wrong people.

"Actually, the last name used to be Markowitz, but when my husband, Lawrence, I know you know his name, since he's the only one who could pay the ransom, anyway, when his grandparents came into America from Russia, they chopped off the *witz*, which made it an easier name, considering what the Jews had to face, though I'm not proud of liking it better, but this was way before Hitler, so who knew how horrible things would get. That's not a problema I think you have here, anti-Semitism. Comprende? Are there any Jews left in México? I don't even know, I'm ashamed to say but..."

"Oh Dios mío. No! No! Cannot be! Your husband is not that name. You are not that name!"

"I most certainly am. Look in mi bolsa, Buenos. All my identification is in there. I was afraid to leave anything in that horrible room. No safe to put things in. So look."

"Oh, no! You are telling truth. You are not Mrs. Solange—"

"Solange St. Sido Mendez Schwartz?! My friend who talked me into going to Vaya Con Dios?"

"Sí. That is the woman I am supposed to take!"

"Oh, my God!"

"Oh, mi Dios. Dios mío! You are the wrong woman!"

"I am the wrong woman!!! Now it makes sense. So, it *was* her ex-husband the Mexican billionaire, Mendez! I thought about it in the closet for a minute when I was trying to figure out why me. Now it makes sense, it all—"

"No, no. That is not the name. No is Mendez. The other name. Señor Schwartz."

"Saulie Schwartz! He's eighty years old and he adores her!"

"No, he is the one who pay my uncle."

"He PAID your uncle!!! Wait a momento. So Your uncle didn't kidnap her, or me, you know what I mean, to get money from Saulie Schwartz? Saulie Schwartz gave *him* money to kidnap Solange?"

"Sí. He no want marriage with her no more. He have other

mujer, well, more señorita. Very young girl. I am very happy to hear it is not your husband who is doing bad thing to you. That was making me very sad and now, my uncle will, no I no say it. This is very bad. I take the wrong mujer."

"Buenos. We are no longer having a Buenos Días. Put away the tequila. We have to think. Wrong mujer. Shit!'

Mimi, Mimi, this is one of those 'on the other hand' dilemmas. You are not the intended victim. However, you know too much and when they realize Solange is still at the retreat, they will hurt her. Oh, God, he's crying. Poor guy, he really messed up.

He's so innocent, he doesn't seem to get it. If Saulie Schwartz paid them, it wasn't to scare her! He paid them to murder her and make it look like a kidnapping! Schleppy old Schwartz? Hot damn. How can anyone trust anyone!

We've got to get out of here, get back to warn her and tell— who? The Mexican police? What did I read about those thirty- five dead people? More. Eleven more bodies found the same week in the same town. HERE!!! Twitter...social media, warned people. Hate it though I may, the Times *said innocent citizens were Tweeting warnings all across the state of whatever this is and everyone is checking before they go out. Maybe Buenos has Twitter? Then it would be public, but he'd have to give up his family and... oh, God, he's scared to death...I have to help him....*

"Don't cry, Buenos. We're in this together and we are going to find a way out of this. But listen, do you think that agua is hot now? If I had a nice hot bath and a few minutes to relax...I think a lot better when I'm clean, then we can come up with a plan, and you can think, too, and we can warn whoever has your kids to get them out of wherever they are, just in case and, by any chance do you have Twitter?"

"Sí. Sí, we all do it now to get updates on where is too dangerous to go. They find cinco heads in front of my children's school and parents warned every one on Twitter so no one go to class."

"Somehow, I don't think that was in the IPO proposal as

one of the marketing strategies. I really think I need that bath now, por favor."

"I go right now and turn the agua on. I never have to think like this before, I too worried about my children and mi tía, she has them. My uncle will kill all of us and you, too, I think Señora Mimi. I am very sorry I make such a mess."

"I'll wait here. I feel a little funny again."

"Okay. Only take a minute now that is water time."

He said they're going to kill all of us! Ay caramba. Where are these phrases coming from, your inner Latina? I am not ready, do you hear that, God? I'm going to be sixty fucking years old next month and I am damn well not going to miss that chance to disintegrate, since my mother died exactly NOW, and never made it! This will not be one of those karmic connection deals… too woo-woo land. First, I'll get clean and then I'll make a plan. If we're going to die, I'm not going to go stinky meek (thank you, Doctor Schlongstein). Guns blazing like Jimmy Cagney in that old movie. "You dirty rats!" Yes, I'll take them with me. (And these guns are where?)

"Señora Mimi, is ready. I put some herbal oils my tía makes in. Is very healing."

"You're a mensch, Buenos. Never mind what it means. Let's go."

"I wait outside. I go on my Twitter and see what they are saying. If anyone knows about the mistaken kidnapping or maybe they still no know it is a mistake. We take you back and I take your friend and my uncle not know."

"Buenos, I'm getting in the tub, okay. But please—I'm not going to set my friend up. And second, Buenos, they do not want to scare her. You have to face that. They were paid to kill her."

CHAPTER
TRES

Hot water. I will never take hot water for granted.... This is so helpful. I'm going to hold my breath and go under and let my hair get clean and I don't care that it will frizz up like, what do the kids call it? A "jewfro." Yes. No more blow-outs, no more straightening. Think of all the time and money I'll save.

Wild, frizzy, maniac hair, and I'll go gray and let it grow down to my ass. Look at me, world! I'm Fucking Sixty.... Okay, Mimi, I think you may be sort of becoming a little unhinged here with all these "gotta be me" brain spasms.

Let's just stay with the next five minutes. Scrub up because you don't know when...you'll...heaven.... It really is true, all the little things are where the joy is, and it's calming me down. Maybe the herbal oils? That tía has great brand possibilities.

Mimi, just get out of the tub and dry off. He put your purse in here, so rinse your mouth and put on some lip gloss, and then you need to talk him into making a run for it.

Whew. Think I overdid it. Feel a little spacey again. Water too hot? Tequila during the day? Or maybe it's the severed heads and the fact that death is a serious possibility that is at odds with your hairstyle-of- the-future plans....

"Señora Mimi. Are you finished?"

"Sí, I'm coming out. But I only have a towel on. I'm feeling very dizzy. Do you have a bed I might...could I just lay down for a couple of minutes? And then we must decide what to do."

"Sí. I open door now. Okay."

"Sí. That was wonderful. I was feeling much better, but now I feel very dizzy."

"Here I help you. My sheets are limpia. Is okay for you. It is right across this hall."

"Oh, it's very cozy. You have nice taste."

"Gracias. My wife, she study designing. She very tasteful. Here you lie down."

"Gracias. I will just close my ojos and rest a minute, but stay. We need to make a plan. Did you have any luck on Twitter?"

"No much. More heads they are finding all over. Many heads. So the tweets are more about where to stay away from. I no know who is doing this. Very, very serio. But no call from my uncle. I send him a text, but he no respond. I think is good, I think he no know I take the wrong mujer or he would call. But I no comprendo what he want now."

"Buenos, I think he will call soon. We should go before he finds out."

"Oh Dios! Is bad, is so bad. I am very afraid. I tell mi tía to take the niños and go to her madre's house and no tell nobody, but he can find anyone."

"Buenos, don't cry. Come here. Let me give you a hug. Have faith. We'll get out of this. There, there."

"No one hold me like this for so long. No madre, no esposa. You are so nice. So soft and beautiful. I no believe you are so old. To be grandmother. You make me feel very, very warm."

Oh, boy, Mimi. This is off the Schlongstein chart. I'm feeling sexy. He's feeling sexy. I'm on a bed in a towel in the house of a Mexican kidnapper young enough to be my son and he's kissing my neck and I'm RAVENOUS.

How long has it been since...? Hard to even remember sexual tension.... No, no.... Yes, yes.... We can't...it's wrong....

But I want you…I want you, too…no, no…yes, yes…sí, sí… Mimi…ay yi yi!

Oh, boy, we should be heading down the highway and—no towel! I am naked! Naked! And he's…oh my, look at that! Never seen a Mexican penis before. Haven't seen any penis other than Lawrence for thirty-five years. Not much basis of comparison, but, whew, it's enormous! And it's so hard! I made this handsome kid's pee-pee shoot up like a cornstalk, well, much cuter than a… oh, God! YES!

"Oh, Buenos, I want you, I want you. Kiss me. Touch me. I'm so hot. I, I…."

"Yo también. You are so soft. Your breasts are so big and sweet, I kiss them. I love them!! Is so long. Not since my wife get sick…."

"Oh, God!"

"Oh, Dios!"

"Yes, yes. Do that. Do it. I want it. Yes."

"Sí. Sí."

"Yes!"

"Sí!"

"Ohhhhhhhhhh. More…oh, oh, oh!"

"Ayyyy, ayyyy. Más, más. Sí. Es so good. You are so sexy."

"Oh, God, Oh. My. GOD.…I'm coming again. Again! Don't stop, please, don't stop!"

"No stop. Más. Más."

"Yes!"

"Sí!"

"What the fuck is going on here?"

"Buenos. Shhh. I'm whispering in your ear now. Not sex, whispering. I can't see the details, but there are three men with guns in the doorway and I think it may be your entire bad kidnapper family."

"No, then it would be four."

"Don't quibble, roll off now, and whatever happens, it was worth it."

"I agree."

"You want to try to explain what you, idiota, estúpido nephew of mine are doing?"

"Uncle, I…it…it no what you think. She is not the mujer. I no make love with a kidnap victim. She is the wrong mujer, so is okay. I wait for your call. You no call, so I no know what to do. She need to go pee pee and have some food and then, I find out, is wrong lady!"

"Yes, it's true! It's all a mistake. But it's not his fault. I think

I know what happened. My friend, who, we think was the intended, uh, victim, she is the one who always goes to the late-night hot-room yoga and then walks down to the Meditation Center, and she always stops at our room, Casita 24, first, to, uh, freshen up, and no one else goes down that path, so there is no way Buenos would think it wasn't her. Not his fault. But she had a past life regression session with Jesus himself, and so I decided to go to her class instead, even though I really hate that stuff, but we paid so much, so, anyway, I was on that path coming from our room and it was very, muy dark, an easy mistake to make and…."

"I want you to shut your fucking bitch mouth or I will cut off those big gringa tits and stuff them down your old whore throat."

"Uncle, she lovely person, no say that."

"What? You fucking donkey head? You're in bed with the victim who could be your mother, humping away on the job, and you no like the way I talk to this cunt?"

"Now, just a minute, Señor Uncle. There is no reason to be rude. We all need to remain calm and solve this problem because we all have a lot to lose."

"Ha, do you see us all laughing? You are very funny bitch. You have a lot to lose and Buenos has a lot to lose, but we have nothing to lose. We have the money for the other woman and now we have you for a ransom. We double our pleasure and profit, I think. This is even better.

"We not even have to go kill the other puta. What her husband going to do? Call the cops! Ha. This is much better."

"Why you no call, uncle? You say you call and then, you no call? Did you know it is wrong mujer and you just making game with me?"

"No, you monkey brain. I couldn't get through because of all those fucking heads they are finding. Good work, but not us, or we wouldn't be here. But we can't go on Twitter or the Internet, too many eyes watching, so I not know anything. But *you* could have sent a message, mierda head. Didn't you look at the picture? This snatch no look anything like the Schwartz one. Schwartz is tall and blonde and very skinny. No tits!"

"Is he saying I'm fat? Gorda? Old, my tits are bad and I'm fat? I'm not fat. Solange is like an ice pick, so by comparison, I guess—"

"No, no, is just his way. Pay no attention—"

"Silencio! Stop this estúpido talking. I ask you a question, nephew."

"I no look at picture because it so dark and she was walking, like you say, and you no say she is with an amiga. If I had known about dos mujeres, I would have been more careful. I make a big mistake, but you say, it work out better, so no harm is happening. Verdad?"

"Oh, harm is happening to you, nephew. Her I need for the ransom call. Get dressed, both of you. No, wait. I want the boys to take pictures of you two. Then we can blackmail her after her husband pays the ransom. Even more fun! So you may live, cunt face. You may live. You do have a husband?"

"Yes. I do, but he's not rich and neither am I."

"Well, that is not good news for you, if it's the truth, but I no think it is the truth. Get dressed, lovebirds. We have enough pictures. Very funny ones, too. Maybe you have kids Buenos's age who will throw up to see their whore mother with this boy."

"I not a boy. I thirty years old. She not old enough to be mi madre. You are sick, uncle. Perdóneme, but this is a nice experience for us."

"Well, actually I am old enough, but we were under a great deal of stress and—"

"Cállate! Shut your boca or I will cut your tongue out and you no be able to lick Buenos's cojones with it, again. Ha ha. Is really very funny, look at your cousins, they are laughing like crazy guys."

"Uncle, por favor, give us some dignity. Let us put on the clothes in privacy or let my brother bring them in and guard us. I no see him, where is Pedro?"

"We no use Pedro for this stuff. He too smart for this stuff, he is our Cyber Guardian. You not know this? He is our Avatar, Pancho Villa. He is at the hacienda trying to get past the policía shutdown of the Internet and the Twitter because of all the cabezas they are finding, like fucking cantaloupes, everywhere! Must be almost fifty heads! They close all the roads, is making this very difficult.

"So he is trying to send e-mail to the Schwartz esposo to tell him job is done. He want a picture of her to prove she is dead, but I will say not possible because of the security and he must send rest of the dinero. But if he don't, we have enough now with this other mujer. These heads, this is the work of the Chili Negros. We not cut off heads. Demasiado GROSS! I don't like all the blood and the mess. Is not us, but the police may be looking for us. Pedro is trying to hack in and find out what is happening."

"He will not be happy if you kill me, uncle. We are brothers."

"He'll get over it or he die, también. Your cousins will bring the clothes. Hey, did your tía make some of those fantastic burritos?"

"Sí. I have many left in the cocina. I can make some and some tequila and…"

"You put on your clothes of shame, we eat, then we go. Your cousin will be right outside the door with his gun on you, so don't even think about making a run."

They have pictures! They are going to hold me for ransom, and then blackmail me with pictures my kids could see! This is not good. Poor Buenos. They won't listen to me, no way, but they can't Google us now, if the systems are down, so he doesn't know I have kids. He's bluffing! That's good. Got to get that camera. Okay. Why am I not hyperventilating? Why am I not panicking? Nothing like a hot bath and how many? I think I stopped counting at EIGHT ORGASMS!

Hmmm. That should be in the kidnap victim's survival guide. I am so relaxed. And my hair is frizzing out. Great! Okay, clothes on. Buenos is dressed. Maybe I can make him feel better.

"Buenos, I think we should be very quiet and play along with them until they take us out of here. All the roads are closed down, so they won't get far, and they can't just kill you with policía everywhere, I don't think so, anyway and...oh, they can't send Lawrence a ransom demand without a phone or something, and they can't mail it because they don't have my address, since I'm the wrong mujer and they won't kill me until they have some money or my ATM pin or, so, I think we're okay for awhile."

"Sí. I think so. But, my uncle is very loco and if he get too frustrated with waiting, he could just kill us for fun. He already have much money from the Señor Schwartz, so I not so sure...."

"Buenos, you come now, bring the bitch, we are going to try and get to the hacienda and make the video for her husband. Move now."

"Okay, I just put away the food and get my jacket and Señora Mimi need to take her purse. She have medicina is important for her asthma."

"Get it. Now. Where is her phone?"

"I have. I bring, but the battery is down. No working."

"Well, we can fucking charge it. Go!"

If they charge it, they will see pictures of Jake and Missy and Abel, and it has all my credit card numbers and addresses and.... But I have my purse. I can cope. Just keep quiet, Mimi. They do not like you. Meek, be meek. It's a challenge, but this is not a Schlongstein sort of situation....

Oh, God, it's a huge Escalade! All blacked out windows. Looks like a B-movie bad men car! The police will stop us, for sure. That's good. I think it's good. How corny. Wouldn't an old, beat-up mini-van with chickens on the roof or something look less suspicious? If it were me, I'd try to be more original and....

"We not taking the Escalade. We take your pickup. Tape them up, Carlos, and put them in the back. Pile all that brush and dirt on them and take off your jackets, mess your hair, put some dirt on your faces. We make it look like we are gardeners coming from a job. Move."

Oh, shit. I'm feeling that cold sweat, pounding heart thing, and I can't get into my purse. Don't want them to think about my purse. He's getting tape. Not the cheap tape! He's got the good stuff. Now I'm scared. Not enough orgasms possible to deal with this. I cheated on Lawrence! I was totally insane. I was shouting 'Do it to me!' Oh God, how truly humiliating. This is the price for a moment of abandon. Buried alive under trash and manure!

"Señora Mimi, don't be frightened. They won't kill us yet. I will be beside you. I have a little knife in my belt. They no search me. I will cut off the tape, but is the good tape, so is not so easy."

"I figured."

"Uncle, I'm putting them in the back. Pancho is loading a wheelbarrow with the brush and dirt. Should be about ten more minutes, and we good to go."

"Faster! We need to get there before it is dark. More patrols at night. Man, that fucking tía's burritos give me gas. We stop at a farmacia and I get some stuff. Vámanos!"

Oh, boy, this is so much worse than the closet, the closet is starting to look very good. Oh, God, where is Taco?? They left the puppy, and I never even put the Neosporin on his ear! My maternal instinct vanished between those sheets!

I'm a really horrible person. I probably deserve to die in the back of a pickup on a highway in México covered with leaves and manure. Probably a fitting end. Shut up, Mimi. You never cut off anyone's head or sold heroin to school children or…. We're moving. What is Buenos doing? He's cutting me out! What a mensch. Air, I can breathe....

"Buenos, when they stop for the stomach medicine, we can make a run for it."

"Sí, I think so, too, but we must be very silent, so they hear nada."

"Uh Oh. We're stopping, and I don't think it's near anything."

"Is a roadblock. Policía."

"I see them. They're wearing ski masks. They have machine guns and big shields, must be for bomb proofing or bullets! But police don't wear ski masks!"

"They do in México, in this part. If cartels see their faces, they come and cut off heads of them and all their relatives."

"I read about this. All the chiefs of police being murdered, and no one will take the jobs. This is awful. I feel so sorry for your people. And the brave officers."

"Not so many brave left. Some very brave, but many work for the cartels, and they just as bad. Nothing is what it seem here. I think is different in America."

"Oh, sure. We just have eighty-year-old Jewish business men paying ruthless killers to murder their very nice wives."

"I entiendo your point. Maybe no place is safe anymore."

"I think that's a healthy way to look at things, at least for the moment. Can you see what's happening?"

"They coming to look. Put the leaves over your face. Do not move."

"Shouldn't we jump up and tell them?"

"Too dangerous. We no know if they good policía or not good. Shhhhh."

What are they doing, poking around with their rifles? Now I understand how hard it must be for all those actors on CSI *to play dead. My nose is itching and I have to pee again. Oh, God, I'm going to sneeze!*

Hold your nose, Mimi! Don't sneeze! But what if they're good cops, and he's wrong? We could be saved right now, and all of this nightmare would end and Lawrence never has to know and I can get back and warn Solange. But if they're not good cops, then they could shoot us or take us and lock us up in one of those Midnight Run *prisons and I'll spend the rest of my life in a filthy cell with rats as big as Tía's burritos and grizzled old lesbians with no teeth and sadistic guards with blackjacks and tequila breath and horrible body odor, scratching off the days of my life with my broken finger nails on the clay wall of my windowless cell and I'll never see Lawrence or Jake or Missy or Abel again. They'll forget all about me, and then I'll contract dysentery and die in a puddle of my own waste. Mimi! Snap out of it!*

We're moving! That's a sign! Now I can sneeze.

"Buenos, can you see anything?"

"A little. The cops, they go. I still have a bad feeling about them. We're not too far from the little mall with the farmacia. There is a small river behind the mall."

"Like a creek?"

"Sí. I think so. What is a creek? This little river, it go for many miles, not too deep or fast, but if we can get down there, we can swim. You can swim?"

"Like a frigging dolphin. High school swim team. Agua ballet...."

"No is necesario to be dolphin or ballerina, just to not drown, is bastante, but very nice to know this about you. I love to swim, myself. I even dive from the cliffs in Acapulco, like the pearl divers, before it got so dangerous there. Lots of heads cut off there. And now the water is very dirty, many pollutions. Very sad to see."

"Yes, so to keep our cabezas, we will slide out of the back of the truck and crawl across the parking lot and then run for the river?"

"I go first, you follow. Maybe we just bend over and run like hell."

"We're slowing down! Are we there?"

"I am looking. Sí, my uncle is going into the parking lot. Shhh. He's going to park and then I think he will come back to frighten us."

"Oh, wonderful. I could really use some more fear. Like Chinese food, an hour later…"

"No comprendo."

"No importante."

"Shhhhhhh. He is coming now."

"Okay, you two. We are past the roadblock. I'm going into the farmacia, but don't think you can get away. My sons are standing right here, with their fingers on their triggers, just in case you have any ideas. Your tía should put a warning label on those burritos; I feel like a fucking fart factory."

"Buenos, it won't work. They have guns and they're right here. We can't risk it. We'll have to wait until we get to his house. Have you been there?"

"Shhh. Whisper even more, I can feel them breathing. One time. Many guards. Many big mean perros, not like Taco. German shepherds, the Rottweilers, the pit bulls, all trained to attack. Very violent."

"Oh, great. SS dogs. Now I'm starting to wheeze. And I can't find my purse."

"I have it. I try to find your inhale machine."

"I just remembered something. I have pepper spray! I brought it on the trip, you know, just in case. I have two in there. We can use it for the dogs."

"He's back, I can hear him farting. I am very sorry, Señora Mimi. I will try to figure out something else."

"Drop the Señora, we're way past that."

"It feel embarrassing to not give you the respect."

"Buenos, you gave me plenty of, respect."

"Ah, sí, I am rojo now. Glad you no can see me."

"We're moving!"

"The hacienda is about an hour from here, if he no take detours. But I think he will go some back way. Don't be worried. The Virgin will help us."

"I'm Jewish. I think I'll let the big G work on this one. But then, again, if she's listening, can't hurt."

"You are funny. I like this way of thinking. I listen to many rich Jewish people at the retreat. They talk so different. Very, more, how I say, opened up and more funny than the others."

"You mean, you've been at the retreat before? I thought I was your first and only kidnapping?"

"Oh, sí. Is verdad, but I work there as security guard, that is how I know my way and get inside and find you. Is my week off, but I know how to get in and out. That is why my uncle pick me to take you, not you, the Señora Schwartz."

"Now I see. Okay, well, we didn't get our swim, so now, I think we must think of something else because when they let us out, they will see we are untaped and they will find your knife and search my purse and find the pepper spray. I'm going to use my inhaler now, okay and then I have to try and calm down again."

"Sí. Yo también. I more scared, now. I try to remember what his hacienda look like."

Oh, my God. I fell asleep! I just took a nap. Are we stopping? This is amazing. I can never take a nap! I can't take a nap in my great big, very expensive bed with silk sheets, central heat and air, no noise, blackout shades. I can't take a nap on a beautiful beach, a porch swing, floating on a pool raft, but I just had a really world-class snooze on a pot-holed Mexican highway, covered with debris and on my way to possible execution.

This is very interesting. I wonder what Schlongstein would think about this. Actually, I don't care what she would think. Hmmm, I may be ready to de-Schlong. We are stopping. Uh oh, dogs. Very loud, barking, growling dog noises. We must be at the hacienda, whatever that means.

"Mimi, we're here! We have to make a plan, very fast."

"I can't believe I fell asleep! Why didn't you wake me up?"

"You were so peaceful. I liked to listen to you snoring."

"Snoring! I don't snore."

"Sí, is cute, little gentle snoring. I like it."

"Well, gracias, but I apologize for sacking out and leaving you alone to figure this out."

"This is what I remember. Is very grande casa. Many rooms. Is a long driveway with big electric gates for security pero no cameras and a guard, but, I think, sólamente uno. I know where the button to open the gate from inside is. If we can get into the front of my truck, I will drive and you can jump out and push the button and we go like hell, no stop. Just go. But this plan only work if they leave us here while they go inside to set up. Sometime, I know he do this. He no know we are out of the tape. And he will have the dogs around. If he leave us, we can run."

"Oh, only the vicious pack of killer dogs! If I jump out, they'll attack me before I can spray their faces; I know I won't be able to face them down, aim, and spray. When I see movies like this, I put myself in the actor's place, and I think I can handle attacking bears, snakes, wild animals. Guess what, I'll freak out."

"Can you drive a stick-shift truck?"

"Uh, no."

"Then you have no choice. You be okay."

"Easy for the guy who stays in the car to say. The camera! Your uncle has the camera with the blackmail pictures! I have to have that!"

"Maybe he leave it in the truck. If he don't, is better to be blackmailed than to be dead, I think."

"You don't know my kids. You don't know Lawrence. Maybe being torn apart by concentration camp dogs isn't such a bad way to go. It has some symbolic irony."

"I no understand. Shhh. He is coming."

"You two, we go and set up. Then we make the tape. Carlos, give her phone to Pedro to charge."

"Buenos, I think they all went in. Can you look?"

"Sí. I no see the guard. The dogs, they are becoming quiet, so I think is okay. I see cinqo perros, but three are wandering off around the side of the house, so only two are near us."

"Which two?"

"One German shepherd. One pit bull."

"Oh, joy. Now I really do need my purse. I have an idea. I can stuff the gummies, for my low blood sugar with my tranquilizers for my anxiety disorder, and we can throw them out and if the dogs eat them, and they will LOVE them, Abel does, the gummies, not the meds, anyway, they will go to sleep or at least slow down enough so we can go."

"This is very smart. Open the purse, we must do this very fast."

"Okay, I'll stuff and you throw them where the dogs are."

"Good, good, but maybe it take too much time to have affect."

"Probably ten minutes, but it's better than having my throat torn out."

"They are eating them all up. You are correct."

"Ay! Buenos, what about the keys?"

"Uncle always leave them in his cars. At least, I hope so. If not, I know how to start."

"Like in the movies?"

"Sí. Is not very difficult. All kids in bad neighborhoods know how to do it."

"Must be a comfort to their mothers."

"You are being…."

"Yep. Can you see anything else?"

"Sí, the guard is coming back."

"Does he have a gun?"

"Of course. But I have my knife."

"And I have the pepper spray, but somehow I don't think it's what we call in America a level playing field."

"Unless I can get behind him and…shhh, I hear something. My uncle is calling to him on the intercom. We are having luck."

"Can you see the dogs?"

"Sí. They are lying down! I think the medicine is working! They no move and the guard is running into the house. Mimi, I think we must do it now. You have the spray, just in case?"

"Yep. You have the knife?"

"Sí. The button to push is on the post beside the intercom. It is red. You must push it hard dos veces."

"Gotcha. Now, I get to say something, I've wanted to say since that really brave guy on the flight that went down in Pennsylvania on 9/11 said before they stormed the cockpit. Buenos, 'Let's roll.'"

"Okay. Uno, dos, tres…jump!"

Up, Mimi, you're up, aim the spray. Dogs, aren't moving. Run. Run. I see the button, even without my glasses. Pretty easy to spot, I guess going out, it's not an issue. Oh, shit, the German shepherd is getting up. He's coming, slowly, but he's coming! Push the button. Twice. Yes. Go around the front. Wait. Buenos could run me over. Don't think. Act. Uh oh, the pit bull is on the move. Didn't one just rip the face off some baby in a carriage in New Jersey? Oy, spray. Mimi! You got him. He's crying. Now I feel bad. In the car. Get back in the car. We're doing this! The gates are opening!

"Buenos. We're out!!! We're free!"

"Look behind. Is no one coming?"

"No, I don't think so. Wait a minute, I hear something. Guns, it sounds like guns? But I don't see anyone."

"I am going off this road. I know secret back way. My uncle, he no know this one. His cars are too grande. We okay."

"Uh oh. Buenos, your uncle has my phone and the camera!"

"Ha. I have a surprise. My uncle he leave the camera. I put it in the back and I take the chip out from your phone, so maybe they don't be able to use it."

"And they don't have me. So they can't send a video. But that means they'll come after us. They have to!"

"Maybe no. There are many risks and many other people to kidnap."

"But I can identify him! I can describe the, the hacienda!"

"Is verdad. But I think he will be afraid to follow you to the Retreat because of Jesus. I think we go back and you get your amiga, and Jesus will help you to go."

"Jesus? But he's just a yoga guru guy."

"I no say more. You no want to know more. But in México, nothing is what it seem to be."

"Oh, no, you don't, Buenos Días-Díaz! None of that subtle shit. If you know something about Jesus, you need to tell me, or I'll be walking into another set-up with my big mouth flapping."

"I am trying to be protection for you. You must swear you will not tell him or your Señora Schwartz what I tell you. Is very dangerous for all of us."

"I swear. I promise, and I never break a promise. Well, once I did, but I was eight years old and didn't quite understand the concept, but not since then, not that I can remember…. So spit it out! What about Jesus?"

"How you think he get the money to build the resort? He not even Mexican and he buy all that land and build the resort and advertise all over the mundo. Have you seen his casa up on the hill? Is muy, muy expensive with movie watching room and pool inside and very high-tech security. How you think he get all this in four years. Is all it has been."

"I have no clue. He's not Mexican? Is he a drug lord?!"

"Almost. He launders the money for the Chili Negros. They are moving into many businesses, banks, restaurants, all over the world. He is their guy here."

"Perfect! Mister holistic-inner-peace-purify-your-body-and-cleanse-your-karma dude works for the head-chopper-offers!"

"Sí. And he smokes."

"HE SMOKES!!!! I love it. I knew he was a phony!"

"Is funny, no? All these people think he is like a god, a great healer, and he's up at his casa, smoking and smoking and drinking big bottles of scotch whiskey, and he is eating KFC all the time. He is crazy for KFC."

"This is so great. This is really going to be a test of my promise-keeping ability. Not the money-laundering, drug cartel-head-chopper-offer part, but the rest is going to be really hard not to blab!"

"Smoking is okay, to tell, but, por favor, wait until you are back in America. I no think any of the people who are crazy for him will believe you. People are very, how do you say, easy to fool."

"That's how you say it. He fucking smokes!

"How far away are we from the Retreat?"

"Not too far now, but the problem is we no have much gas

and I can't use it to go back to the big road and, also, I afraid in case my uncle is out looking for us. So I think, pretty soon we may have to caminar."

"Walk? It looks very…is it all uphill?"

"I think so, maybe some up and then down and then up."

"Oh, even better."

"I go until we are empty, get as close as we can, and then we walk. It will be getting dark, but I have a light."

"I'm afraid to ask how far. *How far?*"

"Maybe ten miles, maybe twenty, I not sure."

"No agua. No gummies, no burritos. This is like a Survivor audition for spoiled, lazy, terrified, aging, Jewish women. Okay. I'm on it."

"Good. You are very strong. More so than you think. We

are getting very empty. Pretty soon we will stop. We are empty now. I pull over. I take the camera and the light. Don't forget your bolsa."

"Not likely."

"We go."

Oh, Mimi, Mimi, now is the time to regret all those spinning classes you almost took, all those almost power walks on the West Side Highway. When's the last time you walked up and down hills for ten miles in the dark? Not even sleep away camp. Not even EVER.

You are not going to be the ONE on the Survivor or the Great Race or even the Apprentice who loses it and gets tossed off during the first round.

You walk or you probably croak. Oh, God, it's really dark and bumpy. Can't see anything. Put on your damn glasses!

"Buenos, I need to stop a minute and put my glasses on. I can't see."

"Here, you take the light. I used to this. I follow you."

"Okay."

The Bataan Death March, Omaha Beach, what about all those kids with cancer and amputees who hobble across America. Keep moving forward. Schlongstein mantra again. The hell with forward! No, don't say that, forward is the only way back. Now that's kind of a cool woo-woo concept. Think about a hot shower. Think about finding Solange and telling her what Saulie has done. Poor Solange. He could hire someone else! No, because we'll, we'll write up a notice, saying if anything happens to her, Saulie Asshole Schwartz did it and send it to the FBI and all those agencies. No! We just threaten to do it so she can still get a nice settlement. YES! Wonder how long we've been going? Ouch! Damn branches everywhere. Ow! Damn rocks in the path. So clumsy. Should have taken those ballet classes with Missy.

"Buenos, how long have we been walking? Are we almost there?"

"Ha. You are so funny. Sarcástico, sí?"

"Um, actually, NO."

"Only twenty minutes."

"Twenty minutes!!! No way. I thought it had been hours. Maybe you should just leave me here, I'll stagger back down to the truck and you can find me tomorrow, unless there are mountain lions or bears or whatever or I dehydrate or have a huge asthma attack or…."

"No, you must come. You can do it. No think about it. We sing. When you sing, you forget everything."

"Yes. You're right. What kind of music do you like?"

"You will laugh"

"No. I'm just praying it isn't Cucaroocoocoo or strolling Mexican guitar songs. I have to tell you, I really hate that stuff."

"No. I like Frank Sinatra."

"No shit! My favorite. I know the entire American Songbook by heart! This is so great. Okay, which song first?"

"How about 'Nuevo York, Nuevo York'?"

"Perfectamente. Ready? Uno, dos, tres—"

"Start a-spreading the news…."

TIME PASSES

"So set' em up, Joe, I got a little story I…."

"Mimi, you are dancing. Be careful. We are almost there, I can see the fences."

"You're kidding me. I'm not even tired. We haven't even done 'Night and Day' yet!"

"I tell you. Singing is good. We walk for almost five hours."

"Frank saved me!"

"Is funny. He is muerto, but he is still so cool."

"So are you, Buenos. Tú también. Gracias. Muchas, muchas gracias.

"Ouch. Buenos! Something just hit me on the head. Really hard! It fell out of that tree. My head's spinning and I've lost my glasses and something slimy is running down my face. Please take the flashlight, tell me what it is?"

"I no think is good idea. I think you will, how you say, 'freak out.' Sit for a moment. I find your glasses."

"Is it blood? What was it, a coconut?"

"I no want to say. Maybe it better you no put on your glasses. We just move fast as soon as you feel okay."

"I want to know. Am I bleeding?"

"Is blood, but no your blood. You okay."

"Buenos, give me the flashlight. I want to see what hit me."

"Is against my best judgments."

"It's a head! A head hit me in the head! A severed head! Buenos, can you find my inhaler? I can feel my airway closing up. Gracias. Better, I'm breathing, but something is weird, well, I mean everything is weird, but look, look at this head! It's a woman, and it's a very upscale head. Look at those highlights! Very pricey work, and, this is sort of catty and mean, but since she is no longer.... I think she's had eyeliner and eyebrow and lip liner tattooing and, hmmm, probably a facelift, fillers for sure, cheek implants? Yep, and look at the teeth. Serious cosmetic dentistry. Buenos, this must be another kidnap victim! Maybe from the Retreat! They decapitated her and dumped her head on this path!"

"I very afraid you are correct. It is not safe here. We must go."

"Buenos, watch out! There's more, ouch, ouch, more heads! Get away from the tree. Look! Oh my God! There must be ten of them!"

"Sí. They put them up in the tree on stakes. Like cannibals. This is not the way the Chili Negros work."

"Then who? Your uncle said he doesn't cut off heads!"

"Sí, but that no mean other members of his gang don't. I think he have many part-time helpers."

"Oh, swell. Beheading on an hourly rate, or maybe a flat fee per head?"

"Mimi, we go now. He must know this road."

"I've got someone else's head's blood dripping down my face, probably crawling with maggots or—Wait! I have hand sanitizer. Keep moving, it's okay, I'll just try and clean this up and not think about it. Sing, we have to keep singing. How about 'My Way'?"

"Is a favorite of mi abuela. I very much love that one."

"I guess we should sing very soft, you know, just in case, and I think we should take a picture, these heads belong to bodies that were real people, and it can help the police, some honest police or some official somewhere to identify them. The Highlight Lady, for sure, someone will be looking for her. I think, maybe, Jesus or one of his people is targeting victims! We have to tell Solange. Go, let's go…"

"'Regrets, I have a few, but then again, too few to mention….'"

"Buenos, maybe that's not the best choice."

CHAPTER
QUATRO

"Señora Mimi—we are here. I open the gate. I have the code. I take you up to your casita, and then I must go. I go back and get Taco, he be so nervioso and he no have food or agua, and then I go to get my family."

"Buenos, you can't go now! You have no gas and you're exhausted. You can't walk back another five hours. You must rest first, and we can tell Solange together."

"No worry. I get some gas here at the staff garage. I be okay."

"No. I'm not letting you go until you eat and rest. Oh, God, we're really here! We actually made it back! A qué hora es? My watch stopped."

"Is almost midnight."

"Solange is probably not even back from the meditation seminar unless she's searching for me or…I didn't even think about that! How ridiculous! She knows I'm missing. There may be police here or, or Lawrence!"

"Is possible. So best I go now. They will take me to the jail."

"No, no, I will tell them you rescued me."

"But, Jesus, he will not believe."

"Jesus has his own ass to cover. I very much doubt he will tell the police anything."

"Unless they are the bad policía and work for the Chili Negros."

"Look, we can't think of everything. You need to rest and we need to eat something and we need to warn Solange and we're going in. I'll go first and check it out, okay?"

"Sí. That is best. Then if something feels mal, you can warn me."

"There aren't any lights on. That's good. Shhh. I'm going to open the door. It's very quiet. Come on."

"I use my light so you can see better."

"Good thinking. No one's here. I'll just turn on a lamp in the bedroom. With the door closed, no one will see it. Wait! I hear some sounds."

"Me, too. I think is the sounds of love."

"No way. She must be having a nightmare. I'm going to open the door."

"No nightmare, she is—"

"Mon Dieu! Jesus! What's happening? Turn on the light! Mimi! It's Mimi! She's alive!"

"Solange, you're alive, too, and—"

"Jesus, s'il vous plaît. Please bring my robe, there is a man."

"Buenos Días Díaz? Qué pasa? What is this?"

"Señor Pilgrim, I bring the mujer back from a kidnapping. She is the wrong mujer. I rescue her."

"Yes! He saved my life! But he's in great danger and, oh, well…. We didn't mean to, uh, break in on your…I mean who could know…. But there are some urgent things I need to discuss with Solange, so, if, since we sort of, ha, broke the mood, anyway, if I could speak with her alone, Señor Jesus, for a few minutes, that would be very helpful."

"Mimi, you can say anything with Jesus here. He is our healer. He cannot see anything but what is true."

"Absolutely, but, Solange, I need to talk to you in private. NOW!"

"Señora Markow, do not allow the fear to overwhelm your spirit truth. I can feel your agitas. This is your ego tremor voice speaking. But I respect this, so I will take Buenos to the hydro-therapy pool and let him detox and then I will provide for his safe return. He is in the hands of the Higher Guides. He will be safe."

"Oh, no. I mean, with all due spiritual reverence and Namaste or Nasty-tasty or May the Force Be with You…and the rest, I don't—"

"Señora Mimi, is okay. I be fine. I should go now. I will write to you."

"But you don't have my e-mail or address, and I don't have yours and what if…you know?"

"I no have a computer no more because of the things you no want to talk about, so you tell me yours and I will not forget for my life."

"Alright, but what if…. Is this adiós?"

"I think so."

"Oh. I hadn't quite gotten this far in my staying-in-the-moment planning and inner fear-mongering. So I guess unless, we went into the Adventure Kidnapping Business together or something, I guess it's the end of…our…."

"Not the end. We are amigos of the heart."

"Now I'm going to cry. So you have to get to some Internet café or something, and let me know you're okay and Taco and your niños. Mimi@Markow.com. Say it back."

"Mimi@Markow…."

"Come now, Buenos. We must get you cleansed and away from here. I will be back, Mimi, to guide you through this transition."

"How about something other than cucumber juice to

ease the spiritual crisis? I am dehydrating and starving as we speak."

"Yes, of course. Solange, open the containers I brought."

"Yes, yes. Of course, mon amour. You are so kind. A bientôt."

"Buenos, we go now."

"Solange! What in the fuck are you doing???? You're sleeping with him?"

"No, it is not what you think. We are in love."

"Love! You've known him for five days, and I've been missing for three of them! And he's, he's.... No, I can't tell you. I swore. This is very hard to digest, especially when I'm gulping air, and I gave all my damn Xanax to those attack dogs."

"Attack dogs? What is this? You must tell me and I will tell you, so much you do not know."

"I'll drink to that, or I would if there was anything to drink. Solange, listen. This is going to really shock you. Sit down. This is a sitting-down kind of conversation. What is that on the table? Champagne? Shame on you. Everyone else is sipping that celery water and…never mind. POUR!"

"But of course, my darling. You cannot know how relieved I am to see you. I was distraught."

"Well, uh, not to seem, as you would call me, cynical, but distraught was not the word that came to mind."

"That is because I have not explained."

"Right. And I will listen to every word. But first, I have to tell you. You are in great danger. It was you they were supposed to kidnap! Saulie! Old Schmucko Saulie paid these very evil people to kidnap you and murder you!"

"Oui. Yes. This is true. I know this. I was very shocked at first, but I see now, it makes all the sense. I was not honest with you, my dear amie. I did not tell you why I wanted to come to this place when there are so many beautiful spas in Europe."

"You said it was because Jesus Pilgrim was a true healer, unlike any of the others and his treatments were the best in the world."

"Oui, I did believe this, but, you know, I do believe too much things that many silly people tell to me, but the true reason is that I think Saulie had someone else, a very young Mexican girl who works here as a masseuse."

"Oh, boy. Well guess what…I know! So how in holy hell would he have met someone like that? He never leaves Palm Beach or Fifth Avenue!"

"It was in Palm Beach. Such negative energy in that place. It began when he and his golfing friends invested with that cochon Madoff, what you call them, a feeder fund, and he lost much, much of his money. So he was full of stress and because he is not French, he does not know how to live with, how you say, the realities of le monde. He become very depressed and so I arranged for him to go to this spa near the golf club where they treat the mind and the body. You know how I am about all of this.

"So he go, and when he come back, he is très, très happy. *Too* happy. And he tell me there is this young lady from the Vaya Con Dios Spa in México who was there to work for the winter and she perform a healing miracle on him. You know this is not the way Saulie talk. So I become suspicious. It is my French womanhood. I know this thing. And also because his turnip is sticking up again."

"His turnip?"

"Oui. Is my name for his wee-wee. Oh, Mimi, you cannot imagine how I hate that old, hairy, yellow turnip! When I marry with him, I have no desire for any more love-making. Monsieur Mendez, he was my fantastic lover. He had the most lovely wee-wee… Like a très joli, smooth, pink banana. But he is not faithful, he is too powerful, too many temptations and his life is in México, and I am longing for Paris, for people of culture. Anyway, you know, I am not young, though do not tell Jesus how old."

"You're safe there. You've never told me."

"Bien. I was very tired then and I did not get but a little bit of money and when I met le Schwartz, I think. Magnifique! He is old and his turnip is dead. Because it was! Fini! And I was his idolized, sophisticated, international wife, his For-Showing-Off Wife. I teach him manners and how to dress and entertain, and in return, I have security and freedom to go where I want and no turnip. But then, after he go with that girl, he come home with special pills she give to him...."

"Viagra? Cialis? The one where you have to be ready to fuck in matching claw footed tubs on the beach or on the stairway right after your grandchildren go home?"

"Non! Is worse. Is some special Mexican compound from here, and his turnip shoot straight up! Every night! This horrible, hairy, yellow...."

"Solange, hungry as I am, that is going to make me hurl. Can you maybe find something else as a wee-wee metaphor, maybe other than fruits or vegetables, though a pink banana isn't so bad...."

"Of course, but I want you to understand how very difficult it was, but what could I do? But then he start to take little trips and he doesn't even want me to, you know, suck his...."

"Solange, I prefer to think of Saulie swinging a putter with his Palm Beach madras slacks on, if you don't mind."

"Je comprends. So I want to come here because I want to see this girl and know how serious this situation is and especially because he has lost so much money. If he makes the divorce, I would be lost! And I am so ashamed that I did not tell you. I was afraid you would give me good advice and I did not want to risk that. I wanted to come and be French with this pouton."

"Sound thinking. So much better than good advice."

CHAPTER
CINCO

"I know it was very silly, but if I had not come, I would not have met Jesus and found true love, when I am so sure that part of my life is fini. So it is always, as Jesus say, 'the universe spinning us toward our destiny.'"

"Solange, I am in a real, I mean, like a MEGA moral dilemma here because I made a promise to Buenos, and his life is at stake, but you are my friend, and I don't think you know anything really about Jesus Pilgrim and right now, what is more important is that Saulie has paid people to *MURDER YOU*!

"So those same people want to re-kidnap me, or you know, *originally* kidnap me since the first time was a mistake; and kill Buenos, and since they took Saulie's money, when he finds out you're alive, he'll hire someone else and we have to do something so he doesn't, you know.... I think I really need some food now, and a shower. I have head-blood on me! Severed head blood!"

"I did not want to say, but you look horrible. I think first you shower and then we finish this talk. I will prepare what Jesus has brought to eat and pour the champagne. But be quick, and do not worry. We will not be harmed."

"Oh, greatly comforting, that Universal Spinning class idea. I am going to take a shower and not look in the mirror."

"I think that is best. I will put fresh clothes out for you."

Okay, Mimi.... Light is on, turn shower knobs. Do not look at mirror. No biggie, since I basically stopped looking in mirrors five years ago. Amazing, how I've learned to put my makeup on and blow out my frizz without actually looking at myself. NO more blow-outs! Yipppee! Now that's my healing work. Yuck! Gross! What is that in the bloody stuff? Better not to dwell on it, though I need to add the head lady to the Solange list of information I can reveal.

What do I do? Betray Buenos? Let her soar off into goo-gooville with a drug laundering/fake Mexican imposter, New-Age creep? I wonder if he knows she isn't rich? I wonder if the Highlight Head was one of his other conquests? God, I'm feeling it all now. I feel about ninety. Everything aches, and I'm so exhausted and hungry and sad and confused and this is not a situation fucking Schlongstein could grasp. So okay, God, do something! What do I tell her?

"Mimi, everything is ready. Come now. We may not have much time before Jesus returns."

"I'm coming."

Okay. I'm clean. I have fresh clothes on. I'm going to eat and I'm going to try and shut up until something makes sense. Listen, Mimi, just listen and stay present. Now I sound like Jesus. Well, he does have some good points, better than Schlongstein just sitting there, probably thinking about how to make a perfect pesto sauce while I'm breast-beating away.

I am definitely quitting therapy if I get out of this. No more blow-outs and no more therapy and also…oh, there's a scale. I wonder if…amazing! I lost ten pounds! So what is the good news here? I lost ten pounds; I had eight orgasms and the best burrito I've ever eaten, and I'm still alive. See, Miss Cynical, even being kidnapped *can* have an upside, then again….

"Mimi!"

"Here, I'm here."

"Très bien. You look, so different. You lose weight, no? And there is a softness in your face, I know that softness, oh, Mimi, mon amie! You make love with the boy! Fantastique! Look, how you blush!"

"I am just red from the hot water. Solange, I am not going to go there!"

"But, of course. I would not think of pursuing. But I am right, no? The first night I was with Jesus and his beautiful golden baguette, I had not remembered what such a look was like, and I saw it in my face, in my eyes. So I understand, without words, ma petite choux."

"Something smells great? What is that? It's KFC, isn't it?"

"Oui. What can I say? Jesus, he adores the fried chicken."

"Extra-crispy?"

"But of course."

"Extra-crispy KFC and champagne. The new healing remedy. Pour!"

"You must promise not to tell the others. It would not look so good."

"I promise. More for us. I'll eat, you can talk. What did you mean about no one harming us?"

"The night they take you away, it is my first time with Jesus, and I didn't come back to the casita until almost dawn and it is time for the morning meditation. So I go to your room to wake you and I see you are not there and I become very worried. Is not like you and also because Jesus tell me that night about a woman in our past life regression workshop who is missing and he is becoming very concerned. So when I found you had not come back, I go to tell to him and he is very upset. Jesus is never upset and he will not discuss with me. He just walk away, as if our night of love is nothing."

"Lots of very expensive highlights, face lift, permanent eyeliner and lip stuff, and enough fillers to stuff a Thanksgiving turkey?"

"You have seen the woman who vanished right before you vanish?"

"Let's just say we bumped heads."

"Mimi, what is this? Tell to me."

"Pour more. Thank you. This is so delicious and I am almost drunk, so promise you won't faint."

"Faint? Je suis Parisienne. Don't be ridiculous."

"Her severed head was up on a stake in a tree on our escape trail, and it fell and bashed me in the head. And there were a lot of other heads. And that old expression, "heads will roll," has a far deeper literal meaning in my mind, now."

"But this is horrible! She is telling in the session about her husband, a very grand Wall Street broker or trader or whatever they are and he is going to jail! That is why she came, to find some strength, and I think the government is stopping all their accounts. She is searching for guidance. But who would know this?"

"Hello? Earth to Solange. Someone at the Retreat is

targeting. There may have been others. Maybe before they didn't actually take them from the premises, so there wasn't a direct connection. I don't know. I took pictures of the heads, but I didn't really look. She, hers was so close and, newly… you know. Pour! I'm shaking all over! Solange, use your still attached you-know-what. It has to be Jesus!"

"Non! I not believe such a thing. Let me finish telling to you what happened."

"Sorry for interrupting. I've probably just signed Buenos's death warrant."

"No! Jesus is a gentle soul. Listen! When he will not talk with me about your disappearing, I do not know what to do. There is no cell service anywhere but at Jesus's chateau and in the office, so I sneak out and go to the spa office, but I do not know how to use the system and then the pouton, Saulie's whore, she come in to give an early massage and she does not know who I am, so I ask her to make a call to Monsieur Mendez in México City. I know his number and she does this and I tell

Mendez, who is still my soul friend, what has happened and he say to me, 'I will make some calls. Do not move from this phone.'

"And so, I wait and the pouton, she go to give the treatment and then she come back, because, of course, she has heard what I say to Mendez and before I can speak a word, Mendez calls and he tells to me what Saulie has done and that you must have been kidnapped by mistake with orders to kill, and I am crying and crying, which I never do, because it makes my eyes all puffed up and my nose red, so for me to cry like that, is very unusual and the girl is watching me and I think she is beginning to see what this is about. Mendez say to me, 'This is the work of a gang called Los Gatos Rojos,' which is the rival to the, something with chilis...."

"Chili Negros?"

"Oui! And he says to me he will call to Jesus Pilgrim and you will be returned unharmed, unless, of course, please forgive how this sounds, Mimi, cherie, unless you are already killed."

"A game changer, for sure."

"It is not funny! My eyes were so puffy, I could hardly see! So then Mendez he say au revoir, and he will make the call and, of course, then I am very afraid because I have had a night of love with Jesus who may be a kidnapper or murderer and so I cannot stop crying and this girl, she give me a cold cloth, which is very good, you know, for the puffy eyes, and we talk."

"She heard everything?"

"Oui, but also I tell to her who I am and what Saulie was trying to do and that I had come there, you know...I tell her everything and, of course, I tell her that Saulie had not much more money and she laughed and then I began to laugh and we made a connection from the universe."

"Very touching, considering."

"I know, is bizarre. But she tell me how she come from this very, very poor family and she grow up on the street and work so hard, selling her body, anything to pay for the school to learn the massage and how meeting Saulie and having this chance to marry with a rich American and, you know, how can I judge? I did the same thing, really.

"But she is very young and very clever and she tell me that when she come back from the Palm Beach, she follow the Madoff case and she see Saulie's name and she realize his money was going away and he would have to pay for a divorce. She, of course, did not know about his plan!"

"And you know this because she *told* you?"

"I believe her. She is not a bad girl. Just desperate, and I understand this. So then we are laughing together about his turnip and she tell me she has found a better old man who has a tiny, little, orange carrot, so she only need to use one half of a pill, sometimes only one third, and the pills are very expensive so with his très petit carrot, she has enough pills to last until he buy for her a condo on the Mayan Riviera, and she already has a new Mercedes and some expensive jewelry, so when he buys the condo, then the pills are fini and she will send him back to his wife. Voilà!"

"Does Saulie know this?"

"Not yet. I tell you, she is smart. She wanted to wait until the deed is signed. But she is very sad about what he has done and she send to Saulie a text message to tell him she know about his evil plan and I am a wonderful woman and they are finished. So you see, he has no reason to kill me now."

"Solange, he still doesn't want to pay for a divorce! You have to tell him you've sent letters to your attorney, so if he tries to harm you, they will arrest him for conspiracy to commit murder! Believe me, if he thinks he can get more pills, he'll find another hungry, little muscle-rubber.

"Actually, he can find one anyway. Baby carrots, hairy turnips, doesn't seem to make much difference. It's the MONEY that draws the honey. Oh, God, I ate an entire bucket of KFC and I'm drunk and I cannot afford to be sluggish or nauseous.

Jesus is going to kill us if Buenos's family, who are the Gatos Rojos, doesn't get here first."

"Non. I must finish telling you what happened here."

"Talk fast and bag the wee-wee metaphors. No mention of any food substances until the chicken settles."

"You are so American. You starve, then you stuff, you never see a French woman eating like that. We are more careful, small portions of very good quality food, to be always chic and elegant and—"

"Solange. No cultural diet tips. We have no time."

CHAPTER
SEIS

"I will be swift. I am very puffy and upset when I leave the girl and I come back to our casita and lock all the doors and I do not know what to do or how to find you and then Jesus he come to the door and I am afraid to let him in, but finally I think I must do what is in his book, 'to trust my inner knowing,' and, Mimi, I *know* he is not a danger to me, so I open the door and he come in and his eyes are puffy, too, though of course he is a man and younger, so it only make him look more handsome and sexy, to see a man vulnerable is so attractive…."

"Speed dial version!"

"Oui. I forget. He tell me everything! The truth of Jesus Pilgrim. He tell me that he is born in San Diego and his real name is the Ernie Finkle...."

"Ernie Finkle!"

"Oui. Well, I believe he say it was the Finklestein, but first he take the end off and then...."

"I get the process. So cut to Life in México...."

"Well, I must tell a bit of his story, so you will not be harsh about him. When he was a boy, he see this movie, it is called *The Falcon and The Snowman* with the Sean Penn playing the Snowman, and he is a rich boy from San Diego family, like Jesus, but Jesus was not yet Jesus, he was the Ernie Finkle, and this character in the film, he is going back and forth into México and dealing the drugs and his friend is Timothy...I forget the last name of the actor who play the Falcon, which is a true story...."

"Hutton. I saw the movie. So Ernie was a border-crossing,

spoiled brat, drug dealer who....”

“Non. You make him sound very bad. He was just young and his family was very difficult and he was raised by a Mexican housekeeper, which is how he speak Spanish so beautifully. But he get into trouble in San Diego and so he go across into México and he find his way to México City and he is, how you say…discovered?”

“Recruited?”

“Oui! Recruited by the chili gang, because he is smart and young and he knows how to socialize and—”

“Deal drugs.”

“Mimi, do not judge. Let me tell you.”

“I’m sorry. It’s my nature, but I’m too bloated to judge, so I’ll try harder to be patient, at least until I see the machete in the doorway.”

"Non! Let me tell you. So, after many years, the chili gang, they move Ernie up, up, up and then, because of the pressure on the police and the government and the Americans, who are always so self-righteous about the drugs and the immigration, the leader of the Chili *Nuevos*?"

"Negros."

"Negros. The leader, he calls a meeting and he tells his people that it is time to cross over into the legitimate businesses, to clean the money and to begin to be real businessmen, and one of the ideas, because of all the Americans who are always looking for the youth and the health cure and the way to sleep well and not have stress; the leader want to open the spiritual spa and then make it a brand, because he say to be a success today, everything must become a brand, and so they will open the spiritual spas everywhere in the country and then in other countries and he has chosen Ernie to be the spokesperson and leader of the spa."

"Every Jewish mother's hope."

"Is great honor. And from there, of course, he change his name and they decide he must write a book, because all of the famous gurus and spiritual stars, they begin with a successful book and so now Ernie is Jesus and he begin to read and think and to write his book."

"Transitions/Transformation?"

"Oui. So he read and he read, all the great wise men of history and he write the book and the chili gang, they build the Vaya con Dios and they have big marketing and the public relations and they know all the editors from all the magazines and many publishers, and voilà!

"The book is released and it become a very famous book and now he is Jesus Pilgrim and he is on the Oprah and the Doctor Phil and he is giving the speeches and workshops all over the world and he is on the blogging and the twittering and the iPhone and the Kindle and all of those things and of course he is also the only one of these healers who is also very chic and handsome and so the women, they adore him and—"

"Solange!"

"Alright. This is the place where you do not understand. And this may be also très tragique for Jesus, because, he becomes transformed. He write this book from his soul and he become a believer and he find that inside of himself is a gift of healing and compassion and it is real!"

"I love happy endings."

"Non! Is not so happy and is not the end! Jesus, he tell the Chili Neeg-ros...."

"Negros. Otherwise it sounds like a racial slur, you know how PC, not KFC, but PC America is."

"Negros. So he tell the leaders who are very, very happy with the success of the book and the spa and Jesus as a brand and they have many plans for the branding with the international companies. For the juices and the Mayan mud compounds and the herbal blends, everything!

"And Jesus, he have a contract for two more books for millions of dollars, even though the chilis take the money, they are promising Jesus many things and of course he is living so well here and is being paid very well, and he is believing that they have stopped doing the bad things.

"No more kidnappings and the drugs and the murdering. He truly believe they are transforming, too. And he even has brought the leaders of the Chili Negros here and he believe they have changed, they have opened their souls to his message—"

"So the drug-dealing, kidnapping, beheading murderers read a self-help book, hug a bougainvillea bush, toss back some pepita seeds, and it's all good."

"Non! That is the tragique part. When I go to Jesus with the story of your disappearing and then my Mendez make calls to him and to the Chili Negros, he must face the horrible truth. They have used him, but nothing else has changed.

"He is distraught! He can see that he is trapped and they

will never let him go and they have everything he has earned. But he is going to protect us and Buenos."

"Whew. Okay, I'm really, really trying to process with your blender and I do, I so do want to believe all this, but, then again, it's sort of 'look who's telling you' and I think it's swell, really swell, if you both have found something special, true love being not so easy to come by, but even so…."

"We have this ritual, when he have to leave me to go to teach or do the business of the retreat, we hold hands and we say, 'I was born when you kissed me, I died when you left me, I lived a few weeks while you loved me.' Is it not so beautiful he tell it to me and my heart paused from beating."

"Humphrey Bogart to Gloria Grahame, directed by Nicolas Ray, very cool film noir, 1950 I think."

"How you know this?"

"I'm a Turner Classic Movie addict and it's sort of a great line. Solange, he didn't write it, but it's still very sweet."

"But he did not say it was from the Humphrey Bogart. Now I am confused."

"Look, this is a long lunch back in the City kind of conversation. Right now, whether he stole a line from a sixty-year-old Bogie movie and he's still Prince Charmant or he's a very clever manipulator isn't the point. I keep trying to make you understand the other gang or cartel or whatever the hell they are, the Gatos Rojos may be coming to really kidnap me and really kill you and we have to get the fuck out of here and find Buenos before his uncle does, so can we put the pause button here until we…. Oh shit! Did you hear that? Someone's at the door!"

"It must be Jesus returning to help us."

"Solange, it isn't Jesus and he's got a gun. Run! The bedroom. Lock the door!"

"There is no lock. It is part of the Overcoming Fear and Isolation teaching. No locks in the rooms."

"I forgot."

"Nobody move. Donde esta Buenos Días Díaz? Is very important I find him. I no want to hurt nobody. I bring the money back."

"What money. Who are you?"

"The money for the ransom of Señora Schwartz. I recognize who you are from the pictures of you with Buenos. In the bed. And I know Señora Schwartz from the photo her esposo send."

"What pictures? Mimi, what does he mean?"

"I have the camera. How can you have seen the…OY! Go ahead and shoot me. I may as well die with dignity."

"No, I no hurt you. My cousin take them on his phone, so I have them at the hacienda muy rápido. Is only my uncle still use a camera. Very old-fashioned. Estúpido."

"Are they coming? Are they here with you? Are you Buenos' brother Pedro?"

"Sí. Is verdad. But I not coming to hurt you. I coming to help mi hermano. I escape and bring the money to show you and Jesus I am not bad."

"But your uncle is going to chop you up, and Buenos and us, too, now that we're all right here like one big piñata party."

"No. You are not in danger. They are all muerto. That is why I come."

"Dead? How?"

"I tell to you and then we look for Buenos. When my uncle and my cousins come with you and Buenos, I am in the special room in the basement behind where they make the videos for the ransoms and the other bad things I cannot talk about. In this room I work on the technology and keep all of the files, so it is secret and I am in there making the blackmail file, so very regretful to tell to you, Señora Mimi, but since I was a boy and my parents are died, my uncle, he take me, and I live in fear and I must do what he say and cannot see or tell nothing to my tía or Buenos and it is breaking my heart because I know mi hermano think I am a bad person, but I am not. I am like my brother. I say to my uncle, 'Take me, I am the oldest, leave one of us to help mi tía.' And so they do it."

"Very noble. And do you happen to have brought that video to prove your nobleness?"

"Sí. I have for you and I have the suitcase with the money from Señor Schwartz for Señora Schwartz. Is much money. Enough for my family to live for their lives. I would not do this if I was bad."

"Pedro, you have just made two gringa mujeres muy contenta."

"Oui! Formidable! It is the spirit of Vaya Con Dios! Monsieur Pedro, cheri, do you happen to know…how much money it is?"

"I think it is one million American dollars."

"No shit! Boy, Solange, he really wanted you dead! I thought he was broke."

"Oh, Mimi, you are so naive. There is broke and there is 'broke.' Broke for Saulie is rich for most people."

"Sí, because that was only half of the ransom, but they no finish the deal because Buenos take the wrong señora and now they are dead, so...."

"I am not greedy. This will be very helpful. Merci beaucoup, but are you positive the rest of the money was not sent, possibly, here?"

"Solange. Think of Highlight Head on a stake in a tree. Greed is not good."

"Oui. You are right. I will be grateful."

"Continue, Pedro, por favor."

"So, Señoras, I am in the secret room and I hear much noise and the dogs are barking and then I hear much gun shots and I am afraid, I no breathe until I almost am passing out and then is quiet. I wait mucho tiempo, until I can hear their cars are going, and finally I open the door and go up the stairs and there they are. Muerto. And the dogs. Muerto, except for the ones outside who are sleeping so in peace. I think they are part of the Chili Negros, because they no are barking or keeping the men away."

"Gummie frogs and Xanax. I guess I kind of saved their lives and believe me, it was not an easy decision."

"I no comprendo, but they are okay and so I take the things and I take a gun and I go. I walk all the way and I pass the heads and I know some of them and I know they are the work of us, Gatos Rojos, not the Chili Negros. Because my uncle he want to be the biggest cartel, he is using many new men, muy peligroso hombres and they are killing many victims and associates, too. And I very afraid that Buenos is one of the heads, but I no see. Where is my brother?"

"We aren't sure. He went with Jesus Pilgrim for something called a detox bath and I don't think he's coming back. Jesus said he would clean him up and help him go back to get Taco and then to see his children and your aunt, so, por favor, Pedro, can you, uh, put the gun away. Even with a bucket of KFC and a lot of champagne in my estómago, it's really making me nervous, like Taco. Okay?"

"I am very sorry. I do not want to make you afraid, but if he is with Jesus Pilgrim, none of us is safe."

"Non! You are mistaken. Jesus send the men to remove your horrible uncle and he is helping your brother."

"Señora, I no think is true. He is not who you think. The American Lady Head on the road? That is not my uncle. That is Chili Negros, and that is Jesus. My brother is not safe."

"Non! It is not like that. Jesus is not even really Jesus. He is an American with name of Ernie Finkle, who became Jesus for the cartel, but then he wrote the book and came to Vaya Con Dios, and he is transformed. He is a healer. He would not do such a thing."

"Señora, I no want to make for you misery, but I know Ernie Finkle. Jesus is not the Finkle. Finkle, he write the book and then Jesus make him disappear. No more Finkle."

"No shit! Are you sure?"

"Sí. I sure. I sorry, ladies."

"Mimi, I need champagne! I am going to faint."

"You need a chair. I'm getting water. And then I think Pedro is right. We've got to get out of here."

"Who is going to get out of where?"

"Jesus! You are here!"

"Of course I am here. And so is Buenos. Look how he

is transformed. Cleared of all the bad energy. Buenos, is that your brother?"

"Sí! Pedro, por favor! Please do not hurt us. Let the women go and I will come back with you!"

"Buenos, it's okay. Your brother has quite a story to tell. He's on our side and he risked his life to come and help you."

"Is the truth, Buenos. Uncle and our cousins are muerto. I bring the ransom and the disc with you and Señora Mimi. I am free, Buenos! And you are alive!"

"Pedro, I want you to give me the weapon. It is making the ladies very upset and it is not in the spirit of what we are doing here. This is a peaceful, healing place. Trust Jesus. Hand me the pistol."

"I cannot do this, Jesus. I know too much."

"Jesus, mon amour, Pedro, he tells to us that you are not the Finkle. That you have the Finkle write the book and probably create Vaya Con Dios and then you do something to him and then you become the leader, but then it is all a lie! I am dizzy with confusion!"

"He is Chili Negro. One of the big jefes! I no give him the gun."

"Whoa! I'm having an asthma attack. Too much deception for my poor airwaves. I'm going to the bathroom to get my inhaler. Please don't shoot or say anything more Magus-like until I get back."

"Magot-like? What means this?"

"No, Pedro. Magus-like. It is the name of a very complicated novel called *The Magus*, where nothing is what it seems. We have the book in our library."

"This is good. Señora Mimi is very smart. We wait. Nobody move."

"Pedro, my son, your hand is shaking. Por favor, you must

trust that I would not hurt you on this mountain where we turn to the Universe, where we practice faith. Has Buenos not told you how we walk over hot coals? We ask our advanced classes to reach into tanks of poisonous snakes to pick out crystals from the bottom. We send them into the mountains without food or water for two days to live as close to their inner power as possible. We conduct a Mayan sweat lodge with the hottest rocks we can find to cleanse all the toxins and fear from their spirits. Would a gun have any place here? Would I harm any seeker who has come to my mountain?"

"I no want to do nothing like that. I see people freak out and people die in that Sedona sweat lodge. Is muy mal. I do not give the gun. This is loco."

"I know this story, mon amour. He is the man with the bad plastic surgery and the fake hair who say to these people he is God and make them worship him as a Spiritual Warrior. I watch this on TV. I did not know you have such things here."

"Solange, there is much you do not know or understand

yet. We have only begun to explore our connection. But to trust in me and me to trust in you is essential. It is true. I am not Finkle. But I did not harm him."

"He's not Finkle!"

"Mimi, are you alright?"

"Much improved and I heard everything. She should trust you? Stick her hands in a snake tank, I saw the *Dateline* on that creep. Buzz cut their hair, stripped them all down to undies or whatever, like the last line into the Dachau pizza ovens. Crouching in that boiling 'lodge' that looked like my four-year-old grandson had built it at his pre-school and three of them cooked to death like human chorizos!" And you're not even Finkle! Solange! Snap out of it!"

"Mimi, you may not believe me, but I care for you. I admire you. You are a highly evolved spirit. You are authentic to yourself. There is a saying: 'a false self has no enemies.' I respect that you are not a pleaser. Speak your truth, even at the risk of your own life, but nothing is quite what it seems, so, please, take some cleansing breaths and look deeper."

"Cleansing breaths did not cut it. It takes steroid breaths to handle this stuff. I am trying not to pass out. But, hey, please continue, Señor Non-Finkle."

"Solange, look at me. I know you. I know so much more than you think and I knew before you came. I know your age."

"But that is impossible! No one…"

"I do. And I know you had your eyes done"

"You had your eyes done?"

"And your breasts lifted"

"You had your breasts lifted?"

"And your hair is not really blond"

"You dye your hair?"

"Mimi, I never tell such things. Is not the French way. Only American women tell to each other all of these private things and then gossip behind their backs. I do not enter into such silliness."

"Very impressive. I'm just surprised because of all our talk about au natural and how vain and shallow American women are and how French men love real women without an age barrier and all…."

"Mimi, I am saying this to Solange so she can feel in her heart that my acceptance of her is not based on her insecurity or need to change who she is. Everyone lies. Everyone here has lied to someone they love about something. It is human nature, but it is our goal to create in Vaya Con Dios, a place where human beings can feel safe enough within themselves and with one another to put aside all those lies. Right now, let us put all the lies we've told to one another aside together before danger comes."

"How about you first, Jesus? Since Solange really has the most to lose right now?"

"It is true I am a leader of the Chili Negros, but I did not harm the lady whose head you found. That was Buenos and Pedro's uncle's cartel. They took her and sent to her husband a ransom demand, but unfortunately for her, it arrived at the same time the IRS and the FBI had just left their apartment with their files and frozen all their accounts. Her husband was in jail, and she ran out of luck.

"And I did not kill Ernie Finkle. I came here to observe and to learn, and the rest of what I told you was true. I became transformed, and I thought this was a good place for me to turn the cartel away from evil. Ernie Finkle was, shall we say, not terribly attractive or well spoken, but he was very well paid and happy to go home. In fact, he changed his name to Ashcanapuri and started his own retreat in Santa Monica."

"Oh, Jesus, my heart is full of pain and doubt. I do not

know what is true. But you are still involved with very horrible men, that is true."

"Yes, it is, but not in the way you think."

"Look, this is way too Inspector Poirot for me. If you're not going to harm us, then get us out of here! Before your bad Chilis get here, or whatever the hell is next."

"That will come. But first we must tell the truth."

"I never lie, Jesus. Well, okay, I blow my hair out and it's really very frizzy, but I've stopped, as you can see and I did betray my husband while in captivity and I want those pictures! And I will *not* show them to him or my children or my dog, so if that's lying, I plead guilty, and that's about it."

"Buenos? Pedro?"

"I no think we have enough of use to lie about. We are really Mexican. We are brothers. We are poor. We do bad thing, but we are not bad people."

"Wait! I hear something! What's that sound?"

"It is a rescue. I think Mendez is sending a helicopter to take us out. He say he will send help. But I cannot go without confessing my lie. I am the biggest of all liars. I cannot judge you, Jesus. You do not know me. Everything is a lie."

"Solange, this may be one of those twitter TMI moments. Let's just get out of here—"

"Non! I must tell my lover and you, Mimi, mon amie. On this mountain. To cleanse my spirit before we go. Jesus, you tell me lies. You say the 'I was born when you kiss me,' and you did not make up this. Mimi saw it in a movie with Humphrey Bogart and you tell to me you are the Finkle, so how can I trust…."

"Mimi saw that movie?"

"Yep, I did. Sorry, whoever you really are."

"Solange, I am truly sorry. I should have told you I didn't

invent those words, but they did come from my heart."

"Oh, Jesus, I am no one to cast the first stone, I am the worst of liars. I am ashamed before my friend Mimi, who is pure of such deception. I deserve to be dead, and I forgive you, Jesus, for whatever lying you have done or wickedness in your past and—"

"Solange! Spit it out. We've got to go!"

"Yes. Yes. I am not Solange! I am not really French. My name is Edy Smithers and I was born in Flagstaff, Arizona."

"Edy Smithers! No fucking way!"

"It is true. I come from white trash drunks. But I was intelligent, and I had always this fantasy to be French, and I receive a scholarship to college and I major in French. So for my junior year, I apply to go to Paris and study at the Sorbonne, and I was accepted. I was reborn! But I am still the Edy Smithers. Then one day, I am sitting in a café reading Colette in French, of course…."

"Oh. My. God. Your name. St. Sido! Colette's mother was Sido!"

"Of course. You know all these kind of things. I always think you would figure that out, but you never ask me about my name."

"I entered with Schwartz and never looked back."

"I will continue…"

"How about continuing without the fake accent…EDY"

"I cannot. It is who I am in my soul. I was reading the *Gigi*, and I look up and I see a group of very lovely young Frenchwomen laughing and having coffee together and suddenly, a woman arrived, waving to them and this woman, she is everything I have dreamed of being. She is blond and very chic, very confident and serene and I hear one of her friends call to her Solange, and my heart is beating so hard and I think, that is who I must be.

"So I copy the way she look and I transfer to the Sorbonne and change my name and I become Solange St. Sido. I believe I am this woman. And then I meet Monsieur Mendez in Paris, and my life becomes what I imagine her life to be. For many years until I leave Mendez, I never even return to America and when I do, it is because I meet a man from New York and so I come and then I meet Saulie and you know the rest of this story."

"Holy shit. This is really amazing. I am speechless. Almost, anyway, though if it makes you feel better, aside from confession being good for the soul, which is, I guess, what Jesus, the non-Finkle was aiming for, I gotta say, you are truly a Solange. You are most certainly *not* an Edy Smithers, and if I was from Flagstaff, not even Tucson or Phoenix, reason enough for fantasy identities and visions of a more glamorous life. Now can we go?"

"Señora Mimi, the helicopter is landed. Everyone come now. Pedro, you must leave the gun. We cannot go with a weapon."

"Buenos, I am afraid, if I leave the gun, Jesus will kill us. He is Chili Negros! He cannot let us go."

"Pedro, you must believe, I will not harm you."

"Pedro, leave the gun. Solange, take the money case. I've got the disc. Get your purse. I'll get mine. Let's go."

"I keep the gun until we get on the helicopter, and then I will drop it."

"Fine. I've just got to pee and grab my purse."

Okay, Mimi, Mimi...just pee. Do not think of how terrified you are of helicopters. Could there be a last lonely Xanax in the bottom of my purse? No time. Shit! This is beyond The Magus, *for sure. Breathe. You are almost free. Unless, of course, lies are layered on lies, and I'm leading the band into mortal danger. How do we know Mendez isn't part of this, or the Chili Negros have sent the chopper or Pedro is lying and the Gatos Rojos are in it, and are going to make a very fancy tree sculpture with all our heads, whoever some of those heads may be. If I get out of this, God, I am going to make Lawrence glue the Witz back onto the end of our name! So into the copter (scary enough) or run like hell. Back down the head trail? Wouldn't have a clue where to go or how to get home. And they would follow me, anyway...so I might as well go with the helicopter. Solange is from Flagstaff! Oh brother.... And we still don't even know who Jesus really is....*

"Señora Mimi, we go now."

"Coming."

Don't overthink this.... You are way beyond figuring anything out now. Move.

"Señora Mimi, ladies will go first. Pedro and I will follow, and he will drop the gun when the machine is off the ground."

"But, Jesus? Are you not coming with us?"

"It is not possible, my love. I must stay here, but I will find you."

"But this is, too unbearable. I will stay with you."

"Solange. Move!"

I'm doing it. I'm in the thing. God, it's so noisy! Looks like just a pilot, good sign. Solange is going to do the Casablanca *good-bye. Okay, she's coming. That's right, up you go, now Buenos. Good. Where's Pedro.... Oh, no!*

"Buenos, look! Pedro and Jesus are fighting over the gun. Jesus has the gun! I knew it. I knew there was more!"

"Do not be afraid. He is bringing him, he is not shooting him."

"He's bringing him with a gun in his back!"

"Lift him in. I tell the pilot to go quick."

"Jesus is coming with him. With the gun!"

"Señor Pilot! Vámos! Immediatemente! El señor tiene un GUN."

"Buenos, can you talk to him? Oh, God, Jesus, don't shoot, please. Why isn't the pilot going?"

"Mimi, mon amie, Jesus will not kill us. I know in my heart. See, he cannot leave me. Mon amour, please, do not take the gun!"

"I need to take the gun, but not for what you think."

"So, why, Jesus? After all that fake farewell drama?"

"Because I think the casita is bugged by the Chili Negros. Now I can tell my lie. I am not a cartel chief. I am DEA, undercover, but it's too risky for me to continue. They are going to figure it out the minute they know I've let you go, so I'm finished here."

"DEA?" If this is true, I want proof! And who then are you?"

"My name is Ramon Sanchez. I was sent to infiltrate the Chili Negros. It's part of a very top-secret plan that the Mexican government has never allowed before, but things are so out of control and the power of the cartels has gotten to be enormous. They're moving into everything. Extortion, terrorism, and not just in México, everywhere. People are dying by the thousands. Journalists, good cops, lawyers, judges are being assassinated. So I was chosen. Here. Look at my ID."

"No shit. Solange, it looks real. Uh oh, guess where he's from!"

"I'll tell her. I was born in Flagstaff."

"Non! It is not possible!"

"Sí. It is. So when I found out who you really were, it already felt like we were fated to be together."

"Sacré-coeur! What are you telling to me? You have known I was born the Edy Smithers? You have known all my lies, before we came together."

"I'm a federal agent. I had to know everything about anyone who could affect my mission, and you were a target. I know everything about you. When you changed your name, you didn't change your passport. It's not very hard to find you out."

"I never think of this. I was very careful to be with people who did not know much about France or ask many questions. In New York, no one cares, it was all power and money and fashion, and in Palm Beach is only the parties and the shopping and the showing off."

"So, now, all the secrets are out. Here's the plan. Pedro, Buenos, we have moved your tía and your kids to another city and given them new identities, just to be extra safe, and I have new documents for you.

"The Chili Negros think you're both dead, or they will soon. We are going to drop you off and refuel and then I'll take Mimi and Solange across the border and get Mimi on a private plane back to New York."

"But what about us, Ramon? I do like this name."

"I've got to go underground, too. I have new passports for us, just in case you want to leave all the past and the deceptions behind and come with me. I never expected to find anyone, the way my life is, but I have a place no one will find us and plenty of money saved up, and if you can take the risk, I want you to come with me."

"And we have the ransom! Yes, yes! I will. I knew it was true. What was in my heart. This is destiny. Not in the book of Finkle, it is our own path."

"This is starting to sound like the end of *As You Like It.*" I think I need an infusion of cynicism from somewhere or I'm going to burst into a very teary chorus of *It's a Wonderful World.*"

"It is, wonderful. Señora Mimi. Is a miracle, and all because of you! If you were not the wrong mujer, none of these miracles would be occurring."

"Buenos, you're the best. Um, *Ramon*, I have to ask you, does my husband, does he know...."

"Nada. It was supposed to be a ten-day retreat with no communication, so as far as your family is concerned, you are sitting in the lotus position and fasting."

"I think I just exhaled for the first time in three days."

TWO YEARS LATER

Senora Mimi, my dear amiga, I ask first that you forgive for me how long I have taken to write this letter. I did not want to write until I could send good news, to make you proud of me and to also send a check for the return of the money you gave my family for the operación on my niño.

I know my tía has told you that he is well and the operación was a success and I know that my tía is now a celebrity in Nuevo York, all because of you and your big Corazon.

I read on her blog that her business, "Tante Tía's Take-Out" is a big success and she is writing (with you) a cooking book and may have a TV show. She tell to me that because there are now almost more Hispanic people in America than any other peoples, that such a show, they think, will be muy popular. This is another miracle you bring to my family.

I now have a computer and I also have big good news to tell to you. I no know if you remember a joke (or sarcastic maybe) you say to me the last night we were together at Vaya Con Dios, when Jesus was taking me away and you say something about "Unless we start a Kidnapping Adventure business, I guess this is good-bye".

Well, I begin to think about this. And I tell Pedro about it and he has some money from all the time with the Gatos Rojos and our tía, who because of you is in America and becoming wealthy, she help us and we begin a business for the rich families who are bored and have children who are bored because they have everything and so nothing is excitement for them.

We called it Kidnapping Adventures and we make a very nice design and advertise it on the Internet and Señora, it has become a big success! Between Pedro and me, we have the experience, and my sister, she know how to give just enough medicina, and we create a very real kidnap experience. The niños love it, sometimes I think, because in the pretending, but making it so real, exchanging of the ransom, they are getting more attention from their parents, but it is not only for the children.

Many adults are looking for some new thrill (like the very, very rich people who pay to swim with sharks or are chasing violent storms or go up in the Space capsules). We even use Taco, which is very good for him. He is becoming a celebrity, too, and we give the Victims autographed pictures of themselves with the Taco, and he even has a tiny little ski mask, which he no like, but he enjoy the compliments and having his picture taken.

I am sending with this some stories about us from the Internet and from 'satisfied customers.' And, of course, we serve tía's famous kidnap victim burritos, chocolate milk for the niños and that nice tequila we have together for the adults.

So now I have saved enough money to provide for my family and to return to you your generosity. Pedro and I know that this will not last for much more time. There is always something new people want, but we are charging much money for this and we will be okay.

Of course there was worry that the Chili Negros and the other cartels, who are coming up all the time, might try to stop us, but it seems the work of Jesus Pilgrim/Ramon Sanchez and his DEA men have broken up the Negros and many of the other groups into smaller less powerful gangs and so far, they are making enough fortunes that they no care.

And we live far away now and with other names, so they no know it is me and Pedro. I hear they like the publicity from the kidnapping adventures because it make it more frightening to the public.

I am writing this to you by my mano, just to be more safe. I think of you todos las días of my life and I will never forget our time together. Oh, uno más thing. My niña, she now have the contact lens and it make her very happy.

So, I say adiós y muchas gracias from mi corazón to you and I send blessings from all of my family to your family. Mi tía she tell to me that your esposo is going to make the production of her cooking program and that you say he is putting down his phone and is talking to you and your marriage is being happy again.

I can not think of any more to tell to you and I know it is a funny way to end, but it is the most from my heart, Vaya Con Dios. If I marry again and have a daughter, she will be named Mimi.

Your amigo,

Buenos Días Díaz

El fin

www.ingramcontent.com/pod-product-compliance
Lightning Source LLC
Chambersburg PA
CBHW020440180626
46812CB00003B/1326